J.

'That settles it

'Hey you two,' ～～～ ～ voice. 'What are you up to?'

We swung round.

A large, red-faced man was just emerging from the back of the garage. It wasn't Sam who's just a shrimp with the face of a dyspeptic ferret. This character looked as if he was rehearsing for the role of Goliath in some biblical epic.

'Scarper!' I hissed.

We turned and fled. Goliath came after us.

J.B. Supersleuth

Jo Dane

RED FOX

A Red Fox Book
Published by Arrow Books Limited
20 Vauxhall Bridge Road, London SW1V 2SA

An imprint of the Random Century Group

London Melbourne Sydney Auckland
Johannesburg and agencies throughout the world

First published by Hutchinson Children's Books 1989
Red Fox Edition 1990

Text © Jo Dane 1990

Made and printed in Great Britain
by Courier International Ltd Tiptree, Essex

ISBN 009 717808

Contents

1
The Stolen Car

My name is Bond. James Bond. Yes, I know what you're thinking. The first reaction is always the same. You hear the name James Bond and you expect to see something tall, dark, handsome and incredibly daring. Instead, before you stands something small, spotty, bespectacled and twelve and three quarter years old. I can't help it. I was in no position to argue at my christening. My father's name was James. So was his father's and *his* father's before that. It's a sort of family tradition. It followed that unless my parents wished to offend all the male line, I must be James also. My parents, in any case, are rather a vague, dreamy couple. They had probably never heard of my fictional, adventurous namesake. And anyway, even if they had, they wouldn't have considered it of sufficient importance to justify altering a long-established family custom.

So here I am. James Bond. A great name to live up to. Only I don't, of course. The original wally, that's me. At least, that *was* me until my second year at Moorside Comprehensive, when I suddenly tumbled into a whole series of amazing adventures. In fact, I almost began to resemble my famous namesake – apart from my spots and specs, that is.

To be fair, I did have a bit of help in my exploits from my best mate, Polly Perkins. I expect you're thinking Polly's a soppy girl, but you're wrong. His name's really Paul, but he's always called Polly, same as I'm usually called JB. It's sort of friendly. Polly's thin and a bit taller than I am and he's got freckles instead of spots. His mum thinks he looks delicate, but actually he's tough as old boots. He lives just round the corner from me, which is handy as we're pretty near inseparable.

I live with my mum and dad and older sister at number seven Sycamore Road. All the roads round us are named after trees. Heaven knows why, as there's hardly a tree in sight. Our house lies just outside a small market town called Elwich, which is about ten miles from the bigger industrial town of Camcaster.

I'm lucky because my parents are really quite normal – for oldies, that is. Dad plays with computers all day in an office, Mum gets cross if I say she doesn't work. I mean, she stays at home and cleans the house and does the shopping and washing and keeps the garden tidy and stuff like that. Oh – and she's a super cook.

Both oldies are a bit old-fashioned, mind you. Not 'with it', if you see what I mean. Strict too. Dad's got the idea that his word is law and nothing was made without him. You can't tell him anything – he knows. Mum's more reasonable, but she tends to concentrate on unimportant things like tidiness and homework. For instance, she often tells me she could keep a bulldozer in full-time use in my bedroom. Still, they're not a bad pair and I'm gradually getting them trained.

But Polly's mum and dad – well! To begin with, they both spoil him and his kid sister, Carol Anne, rotten. That lad's got his own TV, video, computer, music deck – the lot. His bedroom's like the flight deck of the Star Ship *Enterprise*. There are disadvantages though. His oldies are a pair of real fusspots – his mum especially. In addition to which, she's into high-fibre diets and such, which means poor old Polly never gets a square meal like bangers and chips or anything halfway decent. And she's not keen on me at all. In fact, every time I go round to Polly's pad, his mum's welcome approximates to solitary confinement in Siberia. But Polly himself, though not one of the world's great brains compared to me, is a pretty great guy.

However, I was going to tell you how my adventures first began. It was all so simple – the sort of thing that could happen to anyone.

The fateful day dawned just like any other school day – me crunching hastily through my cornflakes and Mum offering useless advice like: 'Time's getting on, James,' or 'Don't talk with your mouth full,' or 'Have you got your dinner money?' Despite her rabbiting on, I galloped out of the house at 8.25 sharp, grabbed my bike, collected Polly at the corner of Laurel Grove, where he lives, and cycled on with him, riding two abreast and chatting happily. At the school gate we were met by Fatso Austin and one or two of his cronies. I'm not too keen on Fatso actually. He tries to take the mickey a bit, but that morning he seemed quite friendly.

'Hi, JB! You get through all the maths homework last night?'

'Yeah,' I said airily. 'No problem.'

'What's the answer to number six then?'

I glared at him.

'That's cheating.'

3

'No, 'tisn't. C'mon, JB. Be a sport. Give us a break.'

His sidekicks sort of edged up each side of me.

'Tell him, JB,' muttered Polly. 'We don't want trouble.'

Fatso's bigger than me, so I gave in and fished my book out of my bag. He scribbled in the answer. I could see at a glance that all his working was wrong so the correct answer wasn't going to fool anyone – least of all old Giggleswick, the maths teacher. The man may look about eighty, but he's bright as a button. I didn't, however, mention this fact to Fatso. I may not be a good fighter but I've heaps of low cunning.

We went into school.

The morning ground its boring way slowly on to twelve o'clock, so completely uneventful that it lulled me into a sense of false security. It was not until we'd come out of the canteen after lunch that Taffy Evans, our head of year, inadvertently started the chain of events that was to alter my life.

Now, Taff doesn't like me particularly. I mean, I can see why really. If you were six foot two of hulking Welsh rugger player would you think much of a spotty nearly-thirteen-year-old who's pure brain rather than brawn? Taff's attitude to Polly and me makes the KGB look paternal. But as our head of year, the man's got power. So when he bellowed 'James' as Polly and I passed the staff room that day, I froze in my tracks and then scuttled back to him, smiling nervously.

'Yes, sir?' I said, smarm side uppermost.

He obviously wanted something because he was

4

trying to smile – and Taff's smile looks as if he's been taught how by some DIY manual.

He handed me a pile of exercise books.

'Just go and put these in the boot of my car, James, will you? It's not locked.'

'Certainly, sir,' I said smartly, seizing the books but dropping one or two in my eagerness to please. Polly promptly retrieved them under Taff's weary gaze and we trotted off.

'Gosh!' whispered Polly. 'He doesn't usually let anyone near that precious car of his.'

Taff's car was his pride and joy. It was a rather super sports job, scarlet and with lots of lights and things. I wouldn't have been surprised to find it had an ejector seat. Taff always parked it in the same place in the staff car park. No one, not even the head, ever dared to usurp Taff's parking space. His car was always polished to a glossy brightness, and sometimes he could be seen giving the thing a surreptitious pat, as if it were a faithful dog. If he'd been in a situation where he had to choose to save either his pupils or his car, we wouldn't have stood an earthly.

We arrived in the car park and galloped up to Taff's space. Then we came to a halt.

The car wasn't there.

'Where is it?' asked Polly.

'How do I know?' I said irritably. 'I'm not psychic. Let's look around.'

We looked around. There were plenty of other cars, but Taff's snazzy red sports job wasn't among them.

'Perhaps he didn't come in it this morning,' suggested Polly.

'He *always* comes in it,' I said. 'Besides, it was here first thing this morning. I saw Taff drive in.'

Polly looked worried.

'What shall we do, JB?'

Polly always looks to me for guidance. It's a pretty big responsibility. I frowned.

'Tell Taff, I suppose. Come on.'

Still lugging the pile of exercise books, we trotted back into school and knocked at the staff-room door. Taffy's face appeared round it.

'Well?'

'Please, sir,' I said humbly, 'your car's not there, sir.'

Taff glared at me. I cowered. Believe me, Taff's glare could put the frighteners on Attila the Hun.

'What d'you mean, not there?'

'It's gone, sir,' I said.

The glare intensified.

'James Bond, if this is your stupid idea of a joke –'

'No, sir,' I said desperately. 'Really, sir, the car's not there.'

Taffy emerged from the staff-room.

'You stupid boys,' he snapped. 'Follow me.'

He swept out. Clutching the books, we scuttled after him like a pair of obedient pack horses.

In the car park Taff came to a halt so suddenly we almost cannoned into him. He was gazing at the empty space where his car should have been. I could have sworn he paled. Then he swung round on us.

'What've you done with my car?' he hissed.

'Me?' To my disgust my voice came out as a strangled squeak.

Honestly, that man would blame me if there was a solar eclipse.

But reason prevailed. Taffy pulled himself together.

'It's been stolen!' he said in a sort of disbelieving whisper. 'Stolen. My car.' He turned back to me. 'Did you see who took it?' he demanded.

I sighed.

'No, sir,' I said patiently. 'There was no car here when we came. Was there, Polly?'

'No.' Polly shook his head violently.

'Right.' Taff came suddenly to life. 'I'll ring the police.'

He turned and belted back towards school. Polly and I looked at each other blankly.

'Gosh!' said Polly again. (Did I mention his vocabulary's pretty limited?) 'Fancy anyone daring to nick Taff's car!'

'Professional car thieves,' I said knowledgeably. 'It's happening all the time. There was quite a column about it in the local rag last week, warning people that car thieves were operating in this area. Hey, there's the bell. Come on, let's ditch these books or we'll be late for French – and you know what Mademoiselle's like.'

Before the end of afternoon school, every kid knew Taff had had his precious car nicked and the police had been called in. We hoped the affair would cause a bit of a diversion and we might be asked to give evidence or something. Fatso Austin even suggested that Polly and I, as vital witnesses, might have to have our fingerprints taken. By home-time, however, when nothing else had happened and we hadn't even caught sight of a single cop, the whole affair began to recede from our minds. As Polly and I set off for home we weren't even giving the matter a thought.

7

'I've got to pick my shoes up from the mender's,' I said. 'I promised Mum. You coming?'

Polly hesitated.

'Well, if we're not too long. Mum gets a bit edgy if I'm late.'

That, I thought, was the understatement of the year.

'It won't take a minute,' I said. 'Let's speed a bit.'

We shot dangerously through the traffic, causing one or two timid drivers to hoot frantically. However, we drew up outside the shop quite safely, although the traffic tried.

I handed over the repair ticket, but Mr Colquhoun, who owns the shop, wasn't there and the moronic youth he'd left in charge couldn't find the shoes. He kept returning to us with varying styles of footwear, saying, 'Are these them?' in despairing tones. Finally Polly and I went round behind the counter to help him. I tracked the right pair down at last and we paid for them and scurried out, leaving the youth to clear up the mess.

Outside it had begun to rain, a slow, steady drizzle.

'We're going to be ever so late,' complained Polly. 'We were *ages* in there. My mum –'

'Not to worry,' I said. 'We'll cut down Gunter's Passage.'

'My mum,' said Polly, 'doesn't like me going down there.'

I glared at him.

'She doesn't like you being late either. And you've no need to tell her we took the short cut. Come on.'

I shoved the shoes in my cycle basket, mounted

and set off in the direction of Gunter's Passage. Polly followed. I knew he would.

Gunter's Passage is a wide alleyway running along the back of the High Street shops, used mainly by delivery vans. It took its name from Gunter's pie shop at the corner – why no one quite knew. But it has been Gunter's Passage as long as I can remember.

At this time in the afternoon it was deserted. We swung into it and put on speed.

We were about halfway down the alley when Polly, behind me, let out a yell. I braked sharply, put my feet on the ground and turned round. Polly drew up beside me. His eyes were wide and startled.

'What's up?' I said.

'I've just seen Taff's car.'

'You've seen what?'

'Taff's car,' repeated Polly. 'In a yard, back there.'

'Where?'

'We just passed it.'

I leaned my bike against a wall.

'Come on,' I said. 'Let's have a dekko.'

We walked back along the alley. Polly came to a stop.

'In there,' he hissed.

'That's the back of Slippery Sam's garage,' I said. 'Dad always says Sam's a crook.'

Slippery Sam's real name is Sam Keogh, but he acquired the nickname 'Slippery' for the obvious reason that everyone *thought* he was crooked, but no one had as yet been able to prove it.

The wide gates to the yard were ajar. We peered through.

A scarlet sports car was sitting in the yard in the rain, rusting audibly.

'See?' muttered Polly.

I hesitated.

'Are you sure it's Taff's? That one's got no numberplates on.'

Polly nodded vigorously.

'I'm s-sure.'

Polly's inclined to stammer a bit when he gets het up, but he's good on cars so I didn't argue.

'Let's have a closer look,' I said. 'Come on.'

Polly wasn't too keen, but I gave him a bit of a shove and followed him into the yard.

We crept up to the car. It certainly looked like Taff's. I peered in through the window. On the front passenger seat was a tiny scrap of torn paper. I pressed my nose against the glass. The paper bore one word pencilled on it: 'MOORS'. The rest was torn away.

'Moorside Comprehensive,' I said triumphantly. 'It's Taff's all right.'

'And look here.' Polly had been rummaging in a pile of stuff at one side of the yard. Now he fished out a numberplate and brandished it. 'This is Taff's numberplate.'

'That settles it,' I said. 'Sam's nicked Taff's car.'

'Hey, you two,' bellowed a voice. 'What you up to?'

We swung round.

A large, red-faced man was just emerging from the back of the garage. It wasn't Sam, who's just a shrimp with the face of a dyspeptic ferret. This character looked as if he was rehearsing for the role of Goliath in some biblical epic.

'Scarper!' I hissed.

We turned and fled. Goliath came after us. I

reached the gate, but Polly, behind me, tripped and went sprawling. He let out a despairing yell as he went down. I stopped and looked round just in time to see Goliath, who'd been right on our heels, catch his foot against Polly's prone body and fall headlong. I heard the crack as his head landed sharply against a concrete post. He gave a funny little moan and went sort of limp. Polly scrambled to his feet. He gazed at the still figure in horror.

'Is he d-dead, JB?'

'I dunno,' I said, 'and I'm not stopping to find out. Let's get out of here.'

'But –'

'Come *on*.' I caught Polly's sleeve. 'There's probably a whole gang in there. Armed, too.'

Polly gave a terrified yelp and almost raced me out of the gate and back to the bikes. We scrambled into our saddles and belted full tilt down the passage.

'What we going to do? Tell Taff?' Polly asked breathlessly.

'No,' I said. 'The police. The nick's in the next street.'

'The p-police?'

'Yeah. Come on.'

Polly, still wittering away agitatedly, cycled after me.

As we chained our bikes to the railings outside the nick (you can't trust anyone these days, can you?) Polly said:

'C-could they charge me with m-murder? If the guy's d-dead, I mean?'

'Course not,' I said, sounding more confident than I felt. 'Just leave the talking to me.'

11

We climbed the steps and entered the police station.

Being a law-abiding type, I'd never been in a nick before and I looked around with interest. There was a sort of bench thing against one wall and, facing it, what looked like a counter with a figure in uniform behind it. I advanced towards him, noticing, as I did so, the three stripes on his sleeve. Obviously a sergeant.

He looked up as we approached and smiled in friendly fashion.

'Can I help you?'

'We,' I said impressively, 'are from Moorside Comprehensive.'

His face dropped like the falling pound. He'd obviously heard of Moorside Comprehensive.

'Well?' he asked sharply.

'Earlier today,' I said, 'one of our teachers had his car nick – er, stolen. He reported it to you.'

'Come to confess, have you?' The sergeant chuckled at his own feeble wit.

I gave him a force-nine glare.

'I came to tell you we've just seen the car. It's in the yard at the back of Sam Keogh's garage.'

The sergeant eyed me doubtfully, but he picked up a pen and reluctantly drew a notepad towards him.

'Your name, laddie?'

'James Bond,' I said.

The sergeant's head jerked up. He was positively snarling.

'Oh, is it? Then I'm Joan Collins. Get out of here, the pair of you. I'll give you wasting police time and –'

'But it's true,' I said desperately.

12

The sergeant raised his hand. I thought he was about to hit me, but he remembered about human rights and refrained.

'Out!' he said briefly.

Honestly, I don't wonder there's so much unsolved crime about. I racked my brains for a way of convincing the oaf.

Suddenly Polly stepped forward. He was tugging something from under his jacket.

'L-look!' he said simply. 'This was in Mr K-keogh's yard.'

It was the numberplate off Taff's car.

We all stared at it, then the sergeant consulted something in a book on his desk, looked at the numberplate again and finally back to us.

'You'd better tell me about it,' he said.

Carefully I related the whole story then I added:

'By the way, when you get to Keogh's place you may find a dead body.'

'What?' snapped the sergeant.

'He may just be stunned,' I explained hastily. 'He was chasing us, see, and he fell and knocked his head.'

The sergeant was looking a bit stunned himself.

'Anything else you feel I should know?' he asked.

'That's the lot,' I said.

He nodded.

'Wait!' he commanded curtly and disappeared through a door at the back.

'D'you think he believed us?' Polly wondered.

'Yeah,' I said. 'That numberplate did the trick. Lucky you thought to bring it.'

'I d-didn't have time to put it d-down,' said Polly simply.

The sergeant returned.

'Right. Thank you, boys. You can leave it to us now. Better give me your names and addresses in case we need to contact you.'

He wrote them down, then looked at me.

'Your name really James Bond?'

'Yes,' I said, going a bit red.

He muttered something that sounded like, 'Poor little devil!'

At that moment the phone on the desk rang and the sergeant picked it up. The worried voice on the other end of the line sounded vaguely familiar. After a few seconds the sergeant said:

'Did you say Paul Perkins?'

Polly jumped nervously.

'It's all right, Mrs Perkins,' the sergeant said soothingly. 'Your son's here with us. . . . No, no, he's not charged with anything. He and his friend came in very sensibly to report something they'd seen. Yes, the friend is James Bond. . . . Yes, madam, they're coming straight home now.'

After a few more minutes during which the agitated yapping from the other end of the line gradually subsided, the sergeant put the phone down and looked at us.

'You'd best get off home. Your parents seem a bit anxious.'

Polly went scarlet. His mum does embarrass him sometimes.

'Well – goodbye,' I said awkwardly.

'Goodbye.' The sergeant smiled at us. 'You've been a big help.'

'Any time,' I said, and shoved Polly out through the door.

We rode home as fast as we could, Polly nattering on about his mum the whole way.

As I entered our house my mother met me in the hall.

'James, what *have* you been up to? I've had Paul's mother on the phone. She said you and Paul were at the police station. She said it was all your fault.'

'She would,' I said bitterly.

'But what happened?'

I thought quickly. My mum isn't as panicky as Mrs Perkins, but you don't ask for trouble, if you see what I mean.

'It was just,' I said, 'that one of the teachers had his car nicked today and when we were coming home we happened to see it – the car, I mean. So we called in at the police station to report it.'

My mother stared at me.

'And they kept you all this time?'

I shrugged.

'You know what they're like.'

When my father came home I had to retell the whole yarn for his benefit. He seemed quite pleased.

'Nice to know you can be sensible for once, James,' he said gruffly.

That, from my dad, is high praise.

Later in the evening a cop called round, not the sergeant but a younger officer, who told us his name was Constable Bracegirdle. He said Sam Keogh had just been driving the car into his garage when the police arrived, so they'd caught him red-handed. They'd also found a couple of other cars nicked previously, though these had been resprayed. The constable sounded pretty chuffed about the whole thing. There was, however, one point still worrying me.

'Was there another bloke at the garage – a big man?' I asked.

I really meant, 'Was he alive or dead?' but you've got to be a bit tactful, haven't you?

'That's right,' said the constable. 'An old customer of ours – Bert Medwin. He'd had a fall and cracked his head, I gather. Not at his best.'

I breathed a sigh of relief.

The constable left soon after that, thanking me and telling me how sharp-witted I'd been to spot the car. I smiled modestly and didn't mention Polly at all.

The real payoff, though, came next morning when Taff thanked us in front of the whole class for getting his car back for him. Instead of glaring at me as usual, he smiled a smile like runny honey and congratulated Polly and me on our prompt action. It's nice when your archenemy is forced to do a bit of grovelling – gives you a sense of divine power, in a way. All the other kids looked most impressed too – even Fatso Austin, and it takes a lot to impress Fatso.

For the rest of the day, kids came up to ask us for the full story, which I kept embroidering a little, till finally rumour was rife that I'd not only recovered the car but knocked out the villains, before delivering them, bound and gagged, to the police. The whole thing made me feel pretty proud, I can tell you.

It did something else. It ended my 'prime wally' image with the other kids. I wasn't JB the wimp any more. I was JB the super sleuth. Even Larry Larkin, who's the head boy and frightfully posh, told me it was a 'jolly good show'! I revelled in the whole thing.

16

Moreover, I now knew what my future career would be. When I grew up I was going to be a detective.

2
The Missing Roman Remains

I mentioned earlier that I have an older sister, but I didn't tell you anything about her. This is because I tend to forget her as she's away most of the time at university. When I say 'university' it's only one of those red-brick jobs actually. Unlike me, she's not really very bright. I intend to go to Oxford – or, failing that, Cambridge.

We don't even see much of her during her vacations – that's her 'in' word for holidays – because she's studying archaeology and she spends most of her leisure hours racing round the countryside digging old stuff up out of the ground, where it's lain peacefully for centuries. It seems a pointless sort of thing to do, in my opinion, and I can't see how a degree in archaeology is going to help her get a job in our world of technological enterprise, which everyone always seems to be yapping on about.

Her name, by the way, is Susan. She's slim and small and very studious-looking – as I am myself, of course. Unlike me, however, she hasn't any spots, she doesn't wear spectacles and she bleaches her mousy hair to a pale blonde.

Shortly after we broke up for the holidays, Susan paid us one of her rare visits. I don't think it was really an acute attack of homesickness that brought her. It was merely the fact that, over the past few weeks, great publicity had been given to the news that some Roman remains had been discovered just outside Camcaster, our nearest large town. The whole area had been fenced off and hordes of long-haired types had descended on the place and were grubbing happily and muddily about, searching for more old goblets and other useless trash.

For Susan, this was apparently too good an opportunity to miss. She arrived home late one night and with a friend in tow. Actually, the appearance of the friend caused problems. To give my sister her due, she had rung up and said she'd be coming, and she was bringing her friend, Evelyn Smythe, another archaeology student, with her.

'That's lovely, dear,' Mum had said vaguely. Then she'd dug out the old camp bed and put it in Susan's room. (We haven't a spare bedroom in our semi-detached hovel.)

Imagine our horror when Susan arrived, accompanied by a six-foot-two hunk of male beefcake. Apparently, Evelyn can also be a man's name, and my sister quoted some old geezer named Evelyn Waugh to prove it. (I'd never heard of him, but both my parents had.) Dad hastily rang the Spotted Cow – our friendly neighbourhood inn – and booked a room for Mr Smythe. Evelyn tried apologizing in his best public-school drawl for being the wrong sex, but I don't think my parents ever quite forgave him.

The next morning, as soon as breakfast was over, Susan roared off in her old souped-up Mini to collect Evelyn and go to the 'dig', as she called it. I went round for Polly, and we spent the morning mooching about and feeling bored. It's funny, you know, you spend the whole of the school term looking forward to the holidays, and then, when they arrive, you don't know what to do with them. Eventually we went down to the brook and tried balancing our way across it on the big sewage pipe. But we both fell in and had to go home to get changed.

When we met again after lunch, Polly said:

'My mum said she'd make me up a picnic lunch tomorrow if I liked. I think it's only to get me out of the way. I'm getting on her nerves, she says.'

'You too?' I said. 'My parents keep asking when I go back to school. It's a very discouraging question at the beginning of a holiday. P'raps I'll get a picnic lunch tomorrow as well.'

'Where shall we go?' asked Polly.

I considered.

'I know,' I said. 'Let's go to the dig.'

'The what?'

'The dig. Those muddy holes where they think the Romans used to live.'

'Near Camcaster? Isn't that where your Susan and her boyfriend are?'

'Yes. P'raps they'll give us a lift.'

'OK,' said Polly. 'I'll tell my mum I'm going looking for Roman remains. She will be pleased. She's always on at me to do something useful.'

'Right,' I said. 'If we can cadge a lift from our Sue, I'll give you a ring tonight and tell you times and everything.'

We spent the rest of the afternoon doing 'wheelies' on our bicycles all round the common. Polly fell off and cut his knee and I accidentally rode into a rock – which appeared big enough to have been left over from Stonehenge – and buckled my front wheel a bit.

It's odd how even the simplest and most harmless of pursuits seems to lead to trouble when time is hanging heavily on your hands.

That evening I announced, over supper, that Polly and I intended to visit the dig next day – and could I have a picnic lunch?

The news caused mixed reactions.

My mother's face lit up at the thought of losing me for the entire day and she happily agreed to pack me some sandwiches and things.

My father said: 'Good idea, James. It's high time you did something useful.'

Susan said: 'We don't want kids.'

'I'm not a kid,' I said indignantly. 'I'll be thirteen this year.'

'You're not coming,' she said firmly.

She promptly found herself in a minority of one. My parents had no intention of passing up this heaven-sent opportunity of getting rid of both their offspring in one fell swoop. Susan, to her disgust, realized they were adamant, not only that I should go, but that she should take both Polly and me in her Mini and return us safely at the end of the day. She was furious.

'What about Evelyn?' she whined.

'Paul and James can sit in the back,' said my mother placidly. 'They're neither of them very big.'

My lack of inches actually causes me great concern and I hate allusions to it. This time, however, it seemed in my own interest to refrain from comment.

When Evelyn arrived at our house later in the evening, I heard Susan moaning to him about taking us. She was obviously seeking sympathy, but she didn't get it.

'But of course we'll take them! I think your brother's a great kid,' came Evelyn's reply.

I smiled sardonically. If he thought to endear himself to any of my family by this sort of comment, the poor sap was sadly mistaken.

I rang Polly with the glad tidings.

'Be round here by nine o'clock sharp,' I said. 'If Sue can get away without us, she will.'

'She hasn't a chance.' said Polly confidently. 'See you, mate.'

'See you,' I said.

Next morning, before nine o'clock, we were both waiting by the Mini like a couple of gun dogs ready for the command to fetch. We both clutched plastic bags containing our lunch. Polly – whose mum is the overanxious type – also had his anorak in case it rained or became chilly. Actually it was a perfect summer day without a cloud in the sky, and even the weathermen hadn't been able to find anything discouraging to say. But Polly's mother believes in being fully prepared for the vagaries of the English climate.

A sulking Susan arrived, bundled us unceremoniously into the back of the car and set off.

On the way, she said: 'I don't want to see you two from when we arrive till when it's time to bring you home. Understood?'

'Understood,' we said happily.

She cheered up a bit after that. We collected Evelyn from his pub and then Polly and I settled down to play noughts and crosses in the back of the car so that we wouldn't have to listen to their learned drivel about layers and metric grids and fosses and artefacts and stuff like that. Honestly, they might have been talking a foreign language.

When we arrived at the dig, Susan promptly decanted Polly and me from the back of the Mini, hardly giving us time to collect our carrier bags.

'See you here at five o'clock,' she said. 'Now vanish.'

We vanished, but not very far. We wandered around the site a bit, looking at all the budding archaeologists working away like denim-clad beavers. They didn't seem to be finding much of anything, for all their efforts. We tried to join in with one group of weirdos who were fiddling about in a trench, but they were most unsociable.

'Go away,' said one fat, hairy type. 'You might damage something.'

Considering that there seemed to be nothing in the trench except some rather unpleasant-looking yellow mud, I didn't see how we could do any really irretrievable damage, but we obediently moved on.

The next couple we tried to help growled: 'We don't want kids,' as soon as we paused by them.

Honestly, I've never met such an unsociable lot.

We just stood around like a couple of spare parts after that, trying not to get in anyone's way and failing very badly. At last Polly said:

'Isn't it nearly time for lunch?'

It wasn't, actually, being only about eleven o'clock, but at least it gave us an aim in life.

'Yeah,' I said. 'Come on, let's go over that ridge and find somewhere away from this mob.'

We wandered off. No one even saw us go. They were too intent on their mud.

On the other side of the ridge, we slithered

downhill a bit, until we came to a spot which looked as if it had been made for picnics. A smooth, grassy slope led down to a river which was chattering away over its little stones. There were a few bushes to give a bit of shade and we had the whole place to ourselves. Not even a sheep in sight.

Happily we settled down and began to unpack our lunch.

Polly gazed enviously at the contents of my carrier bag. My mum, as usual, had behaved as if she were feeding the five thousand after a route march. Cheese sandwiches and sausage rolls jockeyed for position alongside fruitcake, bananas and chocolate biscuits. Sadly Polly unpacked his own mother's offering. I looked at it.

'What on earth's that?'

'Nut cutlets,' said Polly. 'Mum's decided we should all be vegetarians.'

'Never mind,' I said. 'I've got easily enough for two.'

'Thanks, JB,' he said fervently.

We tucked in.

When we had finally finished eating and washed down the meal with a tin of Coke (me) and a carton of pure orange juice (Polly), we lay back replete.

'What shall we do now?' asked Polly.

'Bury all these paper bags and stuff we brought,' I said. 'Remember that telly advert about not mucking up the countryside.'

'How do we bury them? Have you got a spade?'

I glared at him.

'Of course I haven't. I don't usually bring one on picnics.'

'Well, how —'

'Look,' I said. 'See those big stones over there under that bush? If we shift those and then scrape a little hole, we can put the carrier bags in there with any bits in them, then cover the lot with the stones again.'

'Good thinking!' said Polly.

'You do it then,' I said, and lay back on the grass.

He got to work.

After a bit he said: 'I say, JB, there's something here already.'

'So someone else has had the same bright thought,' I said. 'Never mind. Shove our stuff in as well.'

'It's not litter,' said Polly. 'It's – I don't – I'm not sure what it is. Come and look, JB.'

He sounded a bit excited so I began to wonder if he'd unearthed a headless corpse or something interesting in that line. I opened my eyes.

Polly had cleared the rocks. He was tugging at something still more than half buried in the soft soil beneath. I rolled across the grass to him.

'It's coming out,' he gasped.

It did. Rather suddenly. Polly collapsed on top of me.

'Watch it, you clumsy oaf,' I said. 'What've you found, anyway?'

We both sat up to examine our find.

It was a sort of jug thing with a curved handle. An intricate pattern showed faintly through the soil and dirt.

'Been there for some time,' said Polly.

He always was one for understatement.

I took it from him.

'Centuries,' I said knowledgeably. 'This is a Roman pitcher.'

25

'How d'you know?' asked Polly.

I didn't know, of course. My rash statement had been caused by my usual desire to show off. But the more I looked at the thing the more Roman it appeared.

'Let's see if there's anything else,' I said.

There was. A few minutes' eager scrabbling un-earthed a sort of pendant and a broken bit of reddish-coloured pot. That seemed to be the limit of treasure trove.

We sat back and looked at each other.

'That lot are digging in the wrong place,' I said. 'Wrap the stuff in your anorak and we'll go and tell them.'

Polly obeyed.

The muddied weirdos were still delving away dispiritedly when we returned. I spotted Susan and Evelyn and strolled up to them, Polly trotting at my heels like a well-trained puppy.

'Found anything?' I asked casually.

They looked up. Crossly.

'Not a blind thing,' snapped Susan, 'and Main-waring's going to be here at three.'

'Who's Mainwaring?'

'Professor Mainwaring, you clot! He's one of the foremost experts on Roman artefacts in this country. We were hoping to have something really exciting to show him.'

'You're looking in the wrong place,' I said.

'Oh, don't be a fool!'

'But you are. We've found –'

'Oh, Evelyn,' said Susan plaintively, 'get rid of him for me, please.'

The obedient Evelyn leapt out of his hole and seized me by the ear.

'Look,' he said, 'Susan didn't ask you to come here. She didn't *want* you to come. We were forced to bring you. We'll be forced to take you home. But we don't have to listen to your childish prattle. Now, go away.'

'But don't you want to see –'

'I don't want to see anything – including you. Now scarper!' He gave my ear a twist.

We scarpered.

'They're not even interested,' I said bitterly. 'The find of the century – and they couldn't care less!'

'I've had the Romans for today,' said Polly suddenly. 'Let's go down to that river we saw and build a dam.'

'Might as well,' I said.

We trotted off.

As we surmounted the ridge and began to slither down towards the river, we saw we were no longer alone. A fisherman sat on a small stool on the river bank, rod in one hand and a sandwich in the other. There was a basket on the bank beside him. He looked round at our somewhat noisy approach.

'Hello,' he said. 'What are you two up to?'

It's amazing that adults always think you're up to something.

'We've been looking for Roman remains,' I said.

He was quite an old gentleman – fully fifty-five, I should think – but he seemed comparatively friendly and he had very twinkly blue eyes, even though the eyebrows looked a bit fierce and bristly.

'Roman remains, eh?' he said. 'I hope you've had more luck than I'm having with the fish.'

'We have,' I said.

He laughed.

'And what might your name be, young man?'

'James Bond,' I said.

'What?'

'James Bond,' I repeated wearily and waited for the usual wisecrack.

But the surprising old gentleman either was not a devotee of Ian Fleming or was more polite than most grown-ups of my acquaintance.

He just said: 'Nice to meet you, James.' Quite solemnly. Then he added in an interested sort of way: 'Did you say that you'd found something?'

'Rather,' I said. 'Show him, Polly.'

Polly unwrapped his anorak and handed me the jug thing. I dangled it in front of the old gentleman, who gave a sort of gasp and held out his hands to take it, like an overanxious nanny reaching for a newborn baby.

'Beautiful!' he exclaimed reverently. 'Really beautiful. And remarkably well preserved.'

'We found these as well,' I said.

I clicked my fingers at Polly and he obediently handed over the bit of pot and the pendant.

The old gent seemed suitably impressed.

'This is marvellous,' he drooled. 'And where did you find these?'

'Just over there,' I said. 'Under those stones.'

'Is there anything still there?'

'The remains of our lunch,' I said. He looked a bit bewildered so I added hastily, 'We buried our lunch papers so as not to drop litter.'

'Very laudable,' murmured the old gentleman. He sounded a bit amused. 'And where are the rest of your group excavating?'

I was just about to say there were only the two of us, when I realized he meant Susan and Evelyn and their lot. So I gestured towards the ridge.

'Over on the other side of the hill.'

He smiled. 'Let us go and tell them what you've found, James Bond, and point out that they are in the wrong place.'

'I hope they believe you,' I said. 'They wouldn't listen to me.'

He smiled even more broadly.

'They'll listen to me, I think.'

We climbed the ridge.

As we approached the now disheartened diggers, those nearest to us paused and looked up.

'Professor Mainwaring,' Evelyn said. 'I'm so glad you could get here. We haven't found anything interesting for you, I'm afraid.'

I kicked Polly on the ankle to make sure he'd noticed the name. So our old gentleman was Professor Mainwaring, was he? No wonder he was in no doubt the poor saps would believe him.

'You're searching in the wrong places, obviously,' the professor was saying. 'Look what these two young men have found on the other side of the hill.'

He brandished the jug thing lovingly in the air. Polly helpfully displayed the pendant and the bit of pot.

'A perfect Roman flagon,' Professor Mainwaring was crooning, 'a bulla and what looks suspiciously like a piece of a cooking pot.'

'What's a bulla?' asked Polly.

I was wondering the same thing but didn't want to show my ignorance.

The professor beamed at Polly.

'A bulla,' he explained, 'was a gold pendant worn by Roman boys of about your age.'

I nodded in a learned sort of way as if I had known that all the time. It's a trick I find very useful in class. It tends to ward off awkward questions.

By this time the whole crowd of them had gathered round us and they were gazing, in respectful silence, at our finds. Evelyn and Susan eyed me with loathing.

'Shall we show you where we found the things?' I asked, ignoring their basilisk glares.

They all followed us meekly.

'I suggest,' Professor M. was saying, 'that you make some tentative excavations in this new area.'

They made affirmative noises and started work. Unfortunately, for the rest of the afternoon, the only things they dug up were Polly's nut cutlets, carefully wrapped in a plastic bag.

It was a very silent drive home. Susan was obviously in a foul temper. She'd even snapped Evelyn's head off and he'd gone all tight-lipped and public school on her.

When we arrived home, Susan prepared to stamp straight off upstairs.

My father, trying to sound all interested and parental (and failing very badly) said:

'Find anything interesting?'

'Not a blind thing,' snapped Susan, flouncing off.

'I did,' I said. 'I found –'

'Susan dear, your tea's ready,' said my mother.

'I don't want any,' Susan whined. 'I'm going straight up to shower and change and then I'm going out again. A few of us are entertaining Professor Mainwaring to dinner at the Spotted Cow.'

30

'So Mainwaring was there, was he?' my father said. 'Pity you couldn't have impressed him with a find.'

'I found something,' I said. 'I found a –'

'Come and have your tea, James,' said my mother. 'And stop interrupting.'

Me interrupting! No one was letting me get a word in edgeways. I gave up and sat down at the table.

'Wash your hands first, James,' said my father.

Honestly, the way my parents concentrate on trivia is pathetic. I obeyed and returned to the table to eat my tea in silence, while my father nattered on about proposed university cuts which had been announced on the television news. It seemed to involve his entire attention. The idea that his own son had been making historic finds all afternoon was ignored.

It was, therefore, quite a shock for my parents when, later in the evening, a reporter and a photographer arrived from the local paper, demanding to see the boy who'd found the Roman remains at the dig that afternoon. Dad couldn't believe it at first, but eventually came round to the idea and even seemed quite proud in a bemused sort of way. I told the reporter my story and he took it all down in a kind of shorthand. Then he said:

'Let's see, laddie, what was your full name?'

'James Bond,' I said.

He looked at me.

'Are you sure?'

'Of course I'm sure,' I said irritably. 'I ought to know. I've been explaining it to people for years.'

He obediently wrote 'JAMES BOND' in block letters, though he still seemed a bit doubtful.

31

'And the friend who was with you?'

I said: 'Polly Perkins.'

'Oh, a girl,' he said. 'I thought it was another boy.'

'Polly is a boy,' I said.

By this time he was looking rather nastily suspicious, so my mother took over with a long, involved explanation which seemed to leave the reporter stunned but happier.

'Could we have a photo?' he asked.

'Of course,' I said.

'What about your friend – er – Polly? Shouldn't he be in it too?'

'He's camera shy,' I said.

I mean, you can't let mere subalterns get above themselves, can you? The newsmen seemed quite content and I was photographed, smiling intelligently and confidently into space.

Our local paper was due out the following Thursday. I got up early and cycled eagerly along to the nearest newsagent's to buy a copy. Then I stood outside the shop to study the report.

The headline read: 'SCHOOLBOY'S ASTONISHING FIND'.

I read on.

The report began:

'Two small children, James Pond and Paula Perkins. . . .'

I sighed. I should have known. Our local paper is notorious for printers' errors. Even Eddie Shah would have difficulty with that lot.

I looked at the photo of myself leering out idiotically from the front page. My spots had come up beautifully. The photographer appeared to have concentrated on them to the exclusion of all else.

I carefully put the paper in the nearest litter bin and rode quietly home.

3

The Murdered Model

It was shortly after the affair of the Roman remains that we were due to go away on our annual holiday. We usually embarked on this daunting expedition as a complete family, but this year my sister had announced that she was going to explore Hadrian's Wall with a party of students – including Evelyn. Honestly, she's so crazy about the Romans it wouldn't surprise me if she started wearing a toga and ate all her meals lying down. As we were renting a cottage this left us with a spare bedroom, so my parents suggested that I might like to ask Polly along for company.

I leapt at this idea. Family holidays are usually pretty humdrum affairs. My dad used to take me around everywhere with him, out of what appeared to be duty rather than inclination, and we bored the pants off each other. With Polly I hoped for rather more freedom, and even, with luck, the odd adventure.

Polly was as delighted as I was, but had some difficulty convincing his mum that the whole thing was a good idea. The poor woman laboured under this misapprehension that I was bad for her son. In fact, given her head, she'd probably have had me stamped with a government health warning. This feeling, however, was counterbalanced by the fact that for seven whole days she would have only her younger child to keep happily amused. But the deal was finally clinched by Polly's father. Polly told me he overheard his dad say:

'Look, dear, I know you'll worry about Paul if he goes, but, if he doesn't go, I'm likely to have a nervous breakdown.'

Polly said that after this remark his mum capitulated and the plan was on.

Our cottage was on Sark, in the Channel Islands. I'd never been to Sark before, and also we were flying as far as Guernsey – and I'd never flown before either. Polly had already travelled by air once, but only to the Isle of Man, so I told him that didn't count.

The flight was dead boring actually. It was cloudy all the time and we couldn't see a thing, but, when we got on the little launch which was to take us from Guernsey to Sark, things got very much better. For one thing it was quite rough, which made it more exciting. Polly was even a bit seasick and my mother turned rather a nasty shade of green, but I felt fine. I decided that, when I grew up, I might be a naval commander instead of a detective.

Our cottage itself was fab. It stood in a field at the top of the steep hill which led up from the harbour, and had all mod cons and things. Polly was most impressed.

'I say, JB, this is brill! And I bet this island is just the place for adventures.'

I'd been thinking the same thing myself – if we could ditch the oldies.

The next morning we got up to cloudless skies and bright sunshine. Even the sea, having done its worst to us the day before, was now like the proverbial millpond. Polly and I gobbled our cornflakes greedily while I tried to plan how we could escape on our own for the day. The problem, however, was solved for me. As we were finishing breakfast, my dad said:

'Your mother and I are planning to drive all over the island in one of those horse-drawn carriages. If that's too slow for you, why don't you hire yourselves bikes and spend the day on your own?'

'That's a super idea!' I said. 'Thanks, Dad.'

'Oh, James,' fussed my mother, 'are you sure they'll be all right?'

'Of course they'll be all right,' said my father robustly. 'Even our James can't get into trouble on Sark. It's a very law-abiding island.'

'Our James,' stated my mother, 'can get into trouble anywhere.'

'Please, Mum,' I said. 'After all, I am twelve and three quarters now. In Victorian England I could have been down the mines or up chimneys by this.'

My mother hesitated, obviously torn between fears for my welfare and the bliss of a whole day without me. Then she smiled.

'I'll pack you up some sandwiches.'

Polly and I exchanged a triumphant grin and galloped off to get ready before she changed her mind.

Equipped with our sandwiches and with money for drinks and ices and things – my parents are really pretty generous when on holiday – we set off to hire our bicycles. This was accomplished without difficulty and by ten o'clock we were riding along the dusty road without a care in the world.

'Where are we going?' asked Polly.

I sighed.

36

'How do I know? I'm a stranger here. Look, there's the post office. Let's see if we can buy a map.'

The lady in charge of the post office proved to have quite a good selection of maps and we were soon on our way again, pausing only to purchase ice cream to sustain us on our journey.

We had a super morning just cycling around and revelling in the fact that there were no cars to get in our way as they do at home. By twelve o'clock we were more than ready for our lunch, so we left the bikes leaning up against a fence and scrambled down a steep little path to some rocks.

'We should have brought our swimming gear,' Polly said.

'We'll do that tomorrow,' I said. 'We can go snorkelling.'

We gobbled our lunch. Mum had catered for the five thousand as usual and we scoffed the lot without difficulty.

'All we need now,' said Polly, with a hiccup, 'is an adventure.'

Honestly, he seems to think they grow on trees or something.

I was looking at the map.

'There's some caves we could explore,' I announced. 'Look – here – see?'

'Oh, good,' said Polly. 'People always have adventures in caves.'

'Only in Enid Blyton stories,' I said severely. 'In real life they get trapped by the tide if they're not careful. We'll leave the bikes where they are and collect them later. It's not far. We climb up the way we came and then follow this little path along the cliffs. Come on.'

Off we went.

After a bit Polly said: 'I can see a bit of beach down there. Let's try and scramble down.'

'The caves are farther on,' I said.

'So what? We've got all day.'

We began to scramble down.

'Oh, look,' said Polly, 'there's people already there. What a pity!'

The beach was gradually coming more into view. We could now see one corner of it, backed by rugged cliffs. A girl was seated on a rock, gazing dreamily out to sea. A few metres away stood a man at an easel. He was painting.

'He must be an artist,' said Polly admiringly.

We slithered on a bit farther.

'She's posing for him,' Polly added helpfully.

Really, Polly's capacity for stating the obvious is unbelievable sometimes.

'I'd guessed that, you moron,' I said.

'Sorry, JB.' Polly sounded suitably apologetic. 'You always tumble to things so quickly. I – Oh, look!'

The 'look' came out as a sort of agonized squeak. Polly was pointing, his mouth and eyes round O's of horror.

I turned to see if the mermaid had fallen off her rock. Then I gasped.

Another man had appeared on the beach within our field of vision. A villainous-looking character he was too, with dark, greasy, overlong hair and a pallid complexion. He was dressed in a navy guernsey, with denim jeans tucked into big boots like wellies. He was shouting angrily, though I couldn't hear the words. But he was obviously very annoyed about something.

He leapt at the artist and knocked him to the ground, then turned his attention to the painting. It seemed he was no art-lover either, because suddenly a knife flashed in the sunlight and he began to rip the canvas to pieces.

Naturally this infuriated the artist, who scrambled to his feet and flung himself at the vandal, only to be felled to the ground again. This time he lay still, with his arms outstretched on the pebbly beach.

The girl who had been posing on the rock let out a cry and jumped down to run towards the fallen man, but the villain seized her in a cruel grip. She screamed, he shouted something indistinguishable, the blade again flashed in the sun. Suddenly the girl was lying in a crumpled heap on the shore, with the hilt of the knife sticking out of her chest and a patch of red staining her white T-shirt.

It was the most terrifying thing I've ever seen.

Polly let out a sort of choke and clutched me. I lost my balance and stumbled forward, dislodging some stones, which rattled down to the rocks below.

Distracted by the sound, the killer looked up. For a moment his eyes met mine, then I turned and fled as fast as my rather short legs would carry me. Polly had already left. With the air of the most agile rat from the sinking ship he was almost at the cliff top. From below us somebody shouted something. I couldn't hear what and didn't stop to find out.

We didn't pause in our panic-stricken flight even when we reached the cliff top. We ran and ran until our breath gave out and we finally came to a halt outside the gate of a large white house.

Polly said: 'D-did you see?'

Why he thought I was running if I hadn't seen, I can't imagine.

'Yeah!' I said. It was all I had breath for.

'A m-murder!'

'Two,' I said.

'T-two?'

'The other man. The one the baddie knocked down. He wasn't moving.'

'He c-could have been unconscious.'

'He looked dead,' I said.

He had, indeed, looked very dead. We gazed at each other.

'What shall we do, JB?' asked Polly anxiously.

Really, the faith he has in me is touching.

'Get away from here, for starters,' I said. 'He saw us, you know. Then we'd better find the constable.'

'Police?' said Polly.

'No police on Sark,' I said. 'But there is a constable.'

'C-constables are police.'

'Not on Sark,' I said. 'Not exactly. Come on.'

We trotted off.

'How do we find this bloke?' asked Polly.

I ignored that. Partly to save my breath but mostly because I hadn't a clue and I didn't want to destroy Polly's illusions.

Eventually we reached our bikes, which were still exactly where we'd left them. I was surprised. The whole thing was so like a nightmare I'd expected them to have disappeared into thin air. No one was in sight. We mounted and rode back the way we had come.

It must have been siesta time in Sark because there didn't seem to be a soul around.

'Will he have a uniform?' Polly asked.

'Who?'

'This constable character.'

'I don't know,' I said.

'Perhaps a sheriff's star,' pursued Polly.

'You've been watching too many Westerns on telly,' I said coldly.

At this moment we rounded a corner and saw a man sauntering along towards us. He looked big and sane and safe.

I brought my bike to a halt. Polly obediently braked also. The man looked at us.

'Hello, boys. Are you lost? Can I help?'

'We're looking for the constable,' I said.

His eyebrows shot up. He had very blue eyes and they looked right through me.

'Are you now? Well, you've found him. I'm the constable.'

'Where's your ID card?' I said.

He laughed.

'Here we take people on trust, lad. What's the trouble?'

'I want to report a murder,' I said.

'Two, probably,' added Polly.

The constable frowned at us.

'What did you say? Are you being funny?'

Really, grown-ups are all the same the world over.

'We've just seen a girl killed,' I said patiently.

'Where?'

I dug out my map and peered at it.

'I'm not sure,' I said. 'There's a bit of my lunch dropped on the first letter of the name. It could be Terrible Bay.'

'Derrible.' The constable was looking where my

41

finger was pointing on the map. The way he said the name it sounded as if it might be French for 'terrible'.

'That's it,' said Polly helpfully.

'Derrible Bay,' repeated the constable. He began to grin. 'Of course.'

He said it as if murders in Terrible Bay were quite commonplace. I began to wonder wildly if that was how the place got its name.

'Well, aren't you going to do something?' I said. The man didn't *look* thick, but this slowness off the mark was very worrying.

He was still grinning in a rather sly way.

'Take me there,' he said.

'Just us?' interrupted Polly agitatedly. 'The man was armed, you know. Aren't you going to call out a posse or something?'

The constable laughed.

'I think we'll manage. Who are you two, by the way? Are you staying on Sark?'

'I'm James Bond,' I said. 'His name's Paul. And yes, we are.'

'James Bond, eh?' The constable sounded even more amused. 'With you along we shouldn't need anyone else. Not with a name like that.'

I sighed. The man was obviously either a joker or the local lunatic. Just our luck.

We approached the cliff top.

'It was over there,' I said shortly.

'Leave your bikes and come on down with me,' he said.

'Down there?' Polly sounded horrified.

I caught him by the arm.

'We can't let him go alone,' I whispered. 'Keep behind him. Perhaps the killer's gone by now.'

'But the b-bodies won't have.' Polly was getting quite hysterical. 'It was horrible. I –'

'Come along,' said the constable firmly.

It was a headmasterly sort of voice. We 'came along' automatically. But we still let him go first.

Slithering and sliding, we made our way down the steep path. The farther we went, the slower Polly and I followed. Eventually the constable stopped to let us catch up with him. We caught up. Reluctantly. The constable had paused at the spot where part of the beach came into view. I hardly dared look down. The memory of that body with the knife sticking up from it was still fresh in my mind.

I looked at the constable. He was gazing down at the shore, smiling in an inane sort of way. He didn't look like an upholder of law and order beholding mayhem on a beach. I stole a cautious glance down. Then I gasped. Polly, who had peered downwards at almost the same moment, let out a startled gurgle and clutched my arm. I didn't blame him.

A girl was seated on a rock, gazing dreamily out to sea. A few yards away stood the artist painting. Even as we watched the villainous-looking type appeared. . . .

I began to wonder if I'd strayed into one of those time loops you keep hearing about in all the best science fiction.

'He's going to kill her all over again!' Polly said blankly.

He did.

The constable made no attempt to stop the carnage. He just stood there, grinning.

Suddenly Polly said: 'So that's it! They're –'

'Shut up,' I said. I'd arrived at the same con-

43

clusion at almost the same moment, but I didn't want him taking any credit for getting there first.

Almost immediately our suspicions were confirmed. From the beach a voice shouted:

'Cut!'

The 'dead' girl sat up and nonchalantly plucked the knife from her shirt. The artist lying outstretched on the beach rolled over and climbed lazily to his feet. The constable looked at us, still grinning.

'They're making a film,' I said flatly.

Polly gave me a reproachful look.

'They are indeed.' The constable sounded amused. 'And they must be good to have taken you two in so thoroughly. Come on down.'

He began to slither down the path again. Shamefacedly we followed.

There were quite a number of people on the beach – some with cameras and things – and a rather depressed-looking group sitting under the overhang of the cliff, out of range of the scene. Probably extras awaiting their cue, I decided.

A young man wearing immense sunglasses, shorts and what my father would have considered a rather tasteless T-shirt, came across to us.

'Hi, Tom!' he greeted the constable. 'Come to see the fun?'

Before the constable could answer, the 'villain' had joined us.

'I know you two,' he exclaimed, pointing at us. 'You're the kids who ran like scared rabbits earlier. We shouted after you to tell you it wasn't for real, but you were up that cliff like greased lightning. Sorry we frightened you.'

I looked him straight in the eye.

44

'We weren't frightened,' I said. 'But we did think it was for real, yes. We were simply running to fetch the constable.'

They all grinned at one another. I knew they didn't believe me, but at least I'd saved face.

'I'll be getting along then, Tony,' the constable said. 'Perhaps these two would like to stay and watch.'

'Watch?' said Tony, who appeared to be in charge. 'They can take part in the next scene if they want. We're just going to shoot the crowd chase. Would you like that, kids?'

'Ra-ther!' I said, while Polly made eager, agreeing sort of noises.

'Right,' said Tony. 'Come on, then.'

He raised a megaphone and bellowed:

'We're going to shoot the crowd chase now. Gather round, folks, while I tell you what to do.'

Everybody gathered round obediently. Except for the constable, that is. He made a hasty departure.

The next few hours were the highlight of my whole holiday. We had to spot the villain escaping and chase him up the cliff path. We didn't catch him though, because he was supposed to trip and hurtle to his death. I was a bit disappointed we didn't see that but it was to be shot later.

We did the scene again and again before Tony was satisfied. Polly and I were right in front of the crowd during the chase too. After all, we'd had plenty of practice on that cliff path. It was great fun and time simply flew.

I decided that, when I grew up, I'd be a film actor instead of a naval commander or a detective.

At last a halt was called and all the extras were told

45

they could go home. Tony thanked us both very nicely and told us the film would be shown on television at Christmas. Something to tell the kids at school to watch out for anyway, I thought triumphantly.

The chief actors were going on to do another scene and I was all for hanging about to watch. But Polly pointed out that it was now after seven o'clock and I realized my mother would be heading straight for a heart attack. So we left, collected our bikes and rode back to the cottage.

My mother was at the door, peering anxiously all round her. 'Wherever have you been?' she screamed as soon as we hove into sight. 'Your father's just gone down to the harbour.'

'Why?' I said.

'To see if your bodies have been washed up,' she said wildly. 'Ride down after him, James. You might catch him before he's gone too far.'

We set off.

Unfortunately we were nearly at the bottom of the steep hill before we saw my father plodding wearily along. We yelled, and he stopped and turned round. He snarled when he saw who it was. We skidded to a halt beside him.

'Where on earth did you get to?' he bellowed. 'Your mother's been worried sick.'

I noticed he didn't mention that he had been at all perturbed.

'We've been making a film,' I said.

'Rubbish!' said my father. 'You haven't even got a camera. Why don't you try telling the truth for a change?'

He began to trudge back up the hill, muttering

bad-temperedly. We wheeled our bikes and fell into step beside him, ready to support him in case he collapsed with heat-stroke or anything.

'We really were helping make a film, Mr Bond,' Polly said tentatively.

My father stopped still to glare at Polly.

'Your mother's right,' he said. 'James *is* a bad influence on you.'

'But –'

I kicked Polly to shut him up. As I say, it's never any use arguing with my dad. He *knows*.

We all plodded up the hill.

Supper wasn't really a very cheerful meal. My father was tired and cross, my mother reproachful. Neither of them was prepared to believe a word we said. They insisted that we were just making excuses and that we should spend the next day on leading reins held in their firm hands. It looked as if the rest of the week was likely to be a dead loss.

Later that night, I lay in bed planning my future career as a film star. I was already looking forward to viewing myself on telly at Christmas. I imagined how sorry my parents would be that they'd disbelieved me when they saw me leading the chase up that cliff path. I also had pleasing visions of the naked envy of Fatso Austin and the rest. It was all very satisfying. Just before I fell asleep I had one final thought. I hoped the film technicians would be able to do something to camouflage my spots.

4

The Adventure of the Arabian Prince

When we returned to school after the holidays, we found that we had a new boy in the form. He was a dark-haired, olive-skinned youth, who turned out to be not only an Arab but an Arabian prince, no less. His name was Prince Mustapha Abdul Akim. We promptly christened him 'Mustard', and, as he appeared pleasant and friendly, accepted him into the fold. He spoke English very well, but a bit as if he had a plum in his mouth, and he proved to know nothing about football – as we found in the course of a scratch game in the lunch hour.

During the afternoon we almost forgot him, but he caused a considerable stir at four o'clock, when we saw this whopping great car, with a sort of coat-of-arms thing in gold on the door, drawn up at the front entrance. A man in chauffeur's uniform, who was sitting behind the wheel, leapt out as Mustard hove into view and opened the car door for him. Mustard just climbed in – as if, for him, this was all part of life's rich pattern – and was driven away.

Polly, Fatso Austin and I, who had been close observers of this phenomenon, stood and gaped at one another. We couldn't have been more astonished if the lad had been whisked off in a flying saucer.

'Gosh!' exclaimed Polly at last.

'His dad must be worth *pots* of money,' said Fatso Austin enviously.

'Rolling in it,' I said. 'These Arab princes are all the same. It's the oil, you know.'

'My dad works in oil,' said Fatso, 'but we haven't got a Rolls and a chauffeur.'

'Your dad only drives an oil tanker,' I said. 'Princes own dozens of oil wells and employ minions like your dad.'

We mounted our bikes and rode home thoughtfully. It was our first practical experience of the unequal way the world's wealth is distributed.

The next morning we hung around the gate to see if yesterday's effort had been a one-off or was to be a regular performance. Sure enough, promptly at ten minutes to nine, the limousine appeared and decanted Mustard. The chauffeur handed him his briefcase.

'Did you see that?' hissed Polly. 'That bloke saluted him. Saluted Mustard!'

'The lad is a prince,' I reminded him. 'Come on, let's go and meet him.'

Mustard greeted us with a beaming smile.

'Good morning,' he said. 'James and Potty, isn't it?'

'Polly,' said my friend loudly.

'I beg your pardon?'

'Polly. Not Potty. It's short for Paul.'

The Prince looked puzzled, as well he might.

'Polly is longer than Paul,' he pointed out reasonably.

'Yes, I know, but it's because my name's Perkins,' said Polly, as if that explained the whole thing.

I noticed he was beginning to shout a bit, as one

tends to do with foreigners, so I thought it best to change the subject.

'Is it true your dad's a millionaire?' I asked.

The Prince transferred his beam to me.

'I believe so. Why?'

'Well,' I said, 'why are you here? I mean, at Moorside Comprehensive? What's wrong with Eton and Harrow and so on?'

The Prince's beam grew even wider.

'My name is down for Eton,' he confided. 'I may go later. But my father wishes me to mix with all types of people and to see how others live.'

'You should get a fair idea here,' I said.

We went into school.

The day began with a bawling-out session from the Walrus, our deputy head.

The Walrus – whose real name is Mrs Wallis – is a widow, Mr Wallis having died some years previously. Rumour has it that life with her had contributed to the wretched man's early demise. You have to be a pretty strong character, believe me, to stand up to the Walrus.

To begin with, she is built on the lines of a double-decker bus, and her habitual dress appears to be made from bell tents discarded by the Scouts and the colour of fog over Manchester. Her nickname, 'Walrus', is partly a play on the name 'Wallis', but partly, it must be admitted, because of her incipient moustache. Added to which she has a voice which would make the early-warning system seem obsolete.

Not a pretty sight, the Walrus, but one to be feared.

We were, she loudly assured us that morning, the

worst children she'd ever encountered in all her career.

'You ain't seen nuffin' yet,' muttered Polly to me out of the side of his mouth.

She noticed him, of course. Which explains why I had Mustapha to myself at break while Polly was a prisoner – writing lines for Mrs Wallis.

The Prince joined me as we made our usual jet-propelled exit from the classroom. He caught me by the arm.

'James, could I speak to you a moment, please?'

'Sure,' I said obligingly. 'Here, have a bacon-and-onion-flavoured crisp.'

Mustapha gazed at the bag as if crisps were against his religion or something.

'Thank you, no,' he said. 'Could we please go somewhere quiet?'

I lugged him off to the far end of the playground, then waited expectantly.

'James,' he said, eyeing me rather doubtfully, 'the other boys say you are a great detective, rivalling even your so famous Sherlock Holmes. Tell me, is this true?'

'Well,' I said modestly, 'I wouldn't describe myself as great – exactly.'

'But you did catch the thieves who stole Taffy's car, didn't you?'

'Oh – that!' I said casually. 'Yeah.'

'And nearly killed one of them?'

'Just knocked him unconscious, actually,' I said.

'And got the car back?'

'Absolutely!' I said.

'So would you work for me?'

I stared.

'Doing what?'

'Finding out who is planning to kill me.'

'Come off it,' I said. 'Who d'you think you're kidding?'

'I am serious, James. There is a plot against me. My father has many enemies. The chauffeur who brings me each day is also my bodyguard.'

'Why d'you need me, then?' I said.

'He is stupid, that one. Besides, we have to pinpoint the source of the danger. For that, I think we need a great detective such as yourself.'

'The police?' I said weakly.

'The English police? Pah!' Mustapha dismissed the entire force with a snap of the fingers. 'They do not believe such things can happen here. "This is England," they say.'

'But why me?' I said.

'Who would suspect a schoolboy of being my protector? You look so innocent, James. And so young.'

I scowled.

'The job would be very well paid,' the Prince added hastily.

'The job would also be very dangerous,' I said sourly.

'But, James, no one will suspect. They will just think we are friends, no more. Then one day – *bang!*'

'*Bang*, I'm dead?' I said.

'No, James, no. *Bang*, you have discovered the identity of these evil men.'

'Men?' I said anxiously. 'Men? More than one?'

'I do not know, James. You will find out.'

'*Very* well paid?' I said.

combined with an exhibition of work throughout the school.

I had begun as a member of the choir, but funny things were happening to my voice and I never knew whether it was going to emerge as a base grunt or a falsetto squeak. Miss Collins, our music teacher, had therefore regretfully dispensed with my services, and, rather than be left out of the celebrations completely, I had volunteered to sell programmes on the night. Polly at once offered his help also and we had now been joined by Mustapha and two giggle-boxes of girls from the fourth year, whose names I could never remember.

The evening began quietly enough. The concert itself was a dead bore, of course, particularly as nothing went wrong, but the refreshments in the interval were super. It was chiefly the thought of these refreshments that had made me volunteer my services. They were always plentiful, of excellent quality and free to performers and helpers. I had been in the choir the previous year and I had remembered those refreshments through twelve, long, mouth-watering months. I had no intention of missing out because of the vagaries of my wandering voice.

Polly and I managed our programme-selling with our usual effortless efficiency, but Mustard was a dead loss. To begin with, the lad was unusually edgy. He kept jumping if anyone spoke to him too suddenly and he seemed incapable of giving anyone the correct change. And when one anxious father tapped him on the shoulder to indicate the fact that he had received no change at all, Mustapha almost jumped out of his skin.

I reasoned that selling programmes must be out of the usual range of activities for a prince, and thought no more about it.

At the end of the evening, Polly and I stayed behind to help put the chairs away and to eat up some of the refreshments which had been unaccountably left over, and then went to the cloakroom for our anoraks. It was lucky we'd brought them as the rain was bucketing down.

'We're going to get soaked riding home,' Polly said.

'Wish we had a Rolls to collect us,' I said. 'Has Mustard gone?'

'I think he must have.' Polly looked around doubtfully. 'I've not seen him since the concert finished.'

As we left the cloakroom, however, the Prince suddenly materialized beside us.

'James, I've got an idea for a super leg-pull,' he said.

'Oh, yes?' I said, reflecting again how swiftly his command of the well-turned English phrase was coming along.

'Have you realized that you and I are the same height as each other?' he asked.

I'd always thought of him as rather small, actually, but now he mentioned it, I recognized that our heights were identical.

'Well?' I said.

'And our anoraks are exactly same?'

'So what?'

'So why don't you go out now to the car, pretending to be me? Just get in, and if he drives off with you, you win the bet.'

'I didn't know there was a bet,' I said.

'There would be no fun without a bet, James.'

'How much?' I said.

'I thought £5.'

I looked at him.

'We're not all millionaires, you know. I haven't got £5.'

'£5 to 5p then. If he drives off with you, I give you £5. If he knows it isn't me before you get in the car, you give me 5p.'

'Done!' I said.

'Don't do it, JB,' said Polly urgently. 'It's silly. It'll only cause trouble. And how'll you get home after?'

I looked at Mustapha.

'How'll I get home after?'

'But that is easy, James. Once he has driven round the corner from here, you tell him of our little trick and he will turn round and bring you back.'

I said: 'And you'll give me five quid?'

The Prince dug into his pocket, fished out a £5 note and wiggled it about enticingly.

'See, James, I have the money here. And I tell you what – if you succeed, I will then instruct my chauffeur, Mohammed, to give you both a lift to your homes on our way.'

'What about our bikes?' asked Polly suspiciously.

Mustapha dismissed the problem with an airy wave of his hand.

'Your bikes will go in the boot.'

'Sounds great,' I said. 'I can just see Dad's face when I arrive home in a Rolls. OK, Mustard, you're on. Is the car there now?'

'It is waiting, yes. I looked a few minutes ago.'

'Right then.' I flicked up the hood of my anorak to

57

facilitate the disguise. After all, the Prince sported neither spots nor spectacles. 'Here I go.'

I trotted out of the front entrance of the school. In the murk of the drive I could see the shape of the Rolls. The sidelights were on and the engine was running softly.

With my heart beating rather fast, I hurried up to the car. The chauffeur, Mohammed, leapt out and opened the door at the back. I averted my face, pulling the hood of the anorak tighter, as if to keep out the driving rain.

I climbed into the car and sank into the comfortable real-leather upholstery.

The door slammed shut. Mohammed returned to his place behind the wheel. The car slid quietly forward.

I'd done it! That five quid was mine.

I sat back grinning. Let him get round the corner, Mustard had said. I hugged myself in anticipation.

The Rolls moved slowly through the school gates and turned left into the road. Along we went to the corner. We rounded it. Now for it. I took a deep breath.

It was then that I noticed that a glass partition had slid into position, shutting me off from the driver.

I tapped on it.

No response. Mohammed's eyes were fixed firmly on the road ahead.

I knocked louder, with the same result.

I got a bit cross at this point. The car was travelling quite fast now. If I didn't get back soon, the Prince might be annoyed, I might not get my five quid and Polly's overanxious parents would probably be sending out a search party.

I hammered on the partition, but Mohammed appeared to be stone-deaf. I wondered if the car was soundproofed.

I tried again, using the heel of my shoe this time. Mohammed went blithely on his way.

It was then that I noticed something else.

I didn't know exactly where Mustard's father lived, but I did have a rough idea. It was a large house, standing in its own grounds on the far side of town. But it was still *in* town. The Rolls now wasn't. We were speeding along a main road with fields on either side. Even as I gazed out, hardly able to take this in, blinds suddenly slid down over the windows, shutting off my view.

For a minute I sat there blankly, my mouth dropping open in astonishment.

The last time I'd seen something like this had been in a film on the telly, when some crooks had captured the hero and were going to kill him.

Kill him?

I suddenly remembered Mustapha saying: 'Find out who is planning to kill me.'

I went quite cold all over and my spectacles slipped down my nose as they always do when I get nervous.

They thought I was Mustapha. I'd walked into a trap intended for the Prince. And, what was more, the Prince himself had set me up. Me! James Bond, supersleuth, was back to being prime wally again.

I thought – bitterly – that my famous namesake would have had no difficulty in getting out of such a situation.

But then, my famous namesake would have been armed with more than a catapult, a penknife and a toy gun.

After a while I became aware that the car was slowing down. I felt my heart jump into my throat and then drop back, with a dull thud, into my boots.

The car stopped.

I cowered in the corner of the back seat. The door was flung suddenly open. Two men, dressed in those long robe things which appear to be full-dress uniform for Arabs, seized me and dragged me from the car. I noticed that neither of them was the chauffeur. I'd never seen these two before in my life.

It was dark and still raining heavily. I made out, though, that the car had stopped on an overgrown drive before some mossy steps leading up to the front door of a house. I remembered how, in films, prisoners always counted the steps to be able to recognize the place later.

I counted the steps.

Five steps.

I was dragged into a hall and towards a half-open door at the far end, through which I glimpsed a brightly lit room.

Don't think I was just passively letting all this happen, mind you. I was struggling every step of the way. I managed to kick one of my captors on the shin and I bit the other one's hand. But they were tough, those fellows. Apart from hissing something that sounded like the Arabic version of four-letter words, they didn't react to my efforts.

In the struggle my hood slid from my head.

I was hauled into the brightly lit room. It was quite large and the long curtains on the window were closely drawn, but I noticed nothing else about it, because I was far too busy noticing the man seated behind a desk facing the door.

He was dark-skinned and looked as if he, too, could be Arabian, although he was in European dress. He had a long scar down the right side of his face and he looked a very nasty customer indeed. As I was deposited in front of him, he raised his eyes and looked straight at me with an expression of what is usually described as gloating triumph.

Then his expression changed to one of bewilderment.

'You are not Prince Mustapha,' he exclaimed.

'No, I'm not,' I agreed helpfully.

'Then who are you?'

'James Bond,' I said.

He had large, dark eyes. Suddenly they flashed fire. I shouldn't have been surprised if forked lightning had shot from them and struck me dead.

'Don't you try to be funny with me, boy,' he said. 'How did you get here?'

I pointed to the chauffeur, who had unwisely followed me (and my escort) into the room.

'He brought me,' I said.

The forked lightning transferred itself to the luckless Mohammed, who appeared literally to shrink and to try to conceal himself behind his chauffeur's cap, which he was clutching nervously.

'Well?' said my questioner, in tones like liquid ice.

'I thought he was the Prince,' Mohammed answered.

The eyes swivelled back to me. Their owner let out a short, unpleasant laugh.

'You thought he was the Prince! This little spotty English schoolboy with his big spectacles!'

'Hey, steady on!' I protested.

I was beginning to get angry. Fooled by the Prince,

61

sneered at by one of his countrymen. There's one thing, though, about losing your temper. It's difficult to be furious and frightened at the same time.

I managed it.

'The hood of his anorak was up,' Mohammed said miserably. 'It was dark. He got straight in the car. I –'

'Fool! Dolt!' said the man at the desk. Then he continued in what I supposed was Arabic. I couldn't understand what he said, but it was quite clear what he meant. And he reduced Mohammed to a quivering jelly.

Then, unfortunately, he remembered me. The forked lightning pierced through me again.

'So,' he said, speaking like the villain in a pantomime, 'they were wise to our little plan. Prince Mustapha has escaped us – this time. But you are here. You have seen our faces. You realize –'

I'm sure that what I was to realize was something highly unpleasant, but luckily he never got round to telling me, because, at that moment, things suddenly started to happen very quickly.

First of all, another robed minion burst into the room without knocking and jabbered something at Forked Lightning which sent him leaping across to the window to peer out. I caught a glimpse of flashing lights outside, then someone began to hammer on the front door.

A voice shouted: 'Police. Open up.'

At the same moment there was the sound of breaking glass from the back of the house.

My two captors loosened their grip. They appeared undecided what to do next. I took advantage of their indecision and dived under the desk. They hardly seemed to notice.

Running footsteps were heard outside. The door of the room burst open and two men catapulted in, flattening the unfortunate Mohammed against the wall. He sort of relaxed and slid down into an untidy heap. While my two former captors were still dithering, they found themselves handcuffed together and shoved against another wall.

Forked Lightning decided to leave – via the window. He flung it open and leapt out. A happy shout from outside indicated that someone had neatly fielded him.

I decided the danger was over and crawled out of my hiding place.

One of the newcomers turned his attention to me. His friend was too busy removing what appeared to be a whole arsenal of weapons from the handcuffed Arabs.

The stranger grinned at me.

'James Bond, I presume?'

'That's right,' I said. 'Are you two SAS?'

'Nothing so glamorous. Just private investigators for a security firm. At present we're employed by Prince Hassan.'

'Prince Hassan?' I said.

Really, my world seemed to be overcrowded at the moment with the cast of the *Arabian Nights*.

'Mustapha's father.'

'Oh!' I said blankly.

We were interrupted by the appearance in the doorway of two policemen – proper policemen this time, in uniform and everything. My new friend turned to them.

'All sewn up here,' he told them in satisfied tones.

'Just cart these three off in your little black van, will you? The charge is attempted kidnap.'

'Kidnap?' I said indignantly. 'Mustard said they were plotting to kill him.'

'Prince Mustapha was having you on. Come on, James Bond. I'll explain in the car.'

'Where are we going?' I asked suspiciously. I'd had enough of being packed into strange cars for one night.

'Police station,' he said briefly.

I decided to trust him. After all, you've got to trust somebody – and the police seemed quite matey with him.

Outside the house several cars were lined up, some with the 'POLICE' sign on top. The two handcuffed Arabs, protesting volubly but incomprehensibly in their own language, were just being loaded into a black van. So was the still unconscious Mohammed. He was going to get a nasty shock, I thought, when he finally woke up.

We got into another car – no 'POLICE' notice on this one. There was already a driver sitting patiently behind the wheel. One of my two rescuers got in beside him. The chatty one came in the back with me.

'How come you found me so quickly?' I said.

'We had a bleeper on the car which was used to take Prince Mustapha to school. His father, who appears to have spies everywhere, got wind of the kidnap plan, and also that his chauffeur was possibly involved, so he contacted us. He wanted to find out who was behind the plot, so we arranged to bug the car. The moment it deviated from the usual route, we knew the plan was on, and followed. Tonight, in any case, was the likely time for them to put the thing in gear.'

'Why?' I said.

'Because, for once, the Prince wasn't leaving the building in daylight.'

'How did you know you'd got me, not him?'

'I gather that a boy called Perkins made the Prince telephone his father with the whole story. Prince Hassan contacted us. We were already pursuing the Rolls.'

'Why did Mustard get me to take his place?' I said. 'He tried to set me up, didn't he?'

'I think, when it came to the point, he panicked. Something made him suspicious that the snatch was to be tonight. His nerve went. Didn't you suspect anything tonight, when he tricked you into pretending to be him?'

I looked him straight in the eye.

'Of course,' I said. 'But I was his minder. He pays well.'

My interlocutor grinned. I don't think he believed me. But it was my story and I was sticking to it.

Suddenly a nasty thought struck me.

'Did Prince Hassan put Mustard up to this?' I asked suspiciously. 'Getting me to take his place, I mean?'

'Prince Hassan,' said my companion solemnly, 'says he knew nothing about you till his son phoned him.'

Well, I thought, that was the Prince's story and doubtless he, too, was sticking to it.

The police station was bursting at the seams when we arrived. I've never seen so many people packed into one small space. Sardines would have gone on strike. To begin with, my mother and father were there – looking bewildered rather than agitated, I observed. Then there were Polly's mother and father with Polly in tow, and Prince Mustapha, who, I noticed with interest, was sporting an incipient black eye. There was also a distinguished-looking gentleman, who turned out to be Prince Hassan.

'James, are you all right? I am so sorry,' Mustard said.

'I'm fine,' I said. 'What have you done to your eye?'

The Prince fingered his damaged eye gingerly.

'Polly did it,' he said, 'when he found out I had sent you into danger. Then he made me ring my father.'

I looked at Polly.

'Thanks, mate,' I said.

Polly blushed.

'Think nothing of it, JB.'

His mother said: 'James Bond, you're a bad influence on our Paul. He never gets into trouble except when he's with you. He –'

The desk sergeant, who had been simmering away unhappily for the past few minutes, now came to the boil.

'If you could all be quiet for a few minutes,' he said loudly, 'perhaps we could get this sorted out, then you could all go home.'

It actually took over an hour to get it all sorted out – statements taken, Prince Hassan placated and Polly's mum pacified. Eventually it was all over and I was loaded into my third car of the evening – my dad's old Ford this time – and driven home.

Over a late supper, I tried to explain the whole thing simply to my poor, bewildered parents, but I don't think I really succeeded.

Two days later a large, imposing-looking envelope, addressed to me, slid through our letter-box. It had the same sort of crest on it as Mustard's Rolls had. Inside was a cheque for £1000, with quite a nice thank-you note signed by someone on behalf of Prince Hassan.

But my luck was dead out. My father made me use the lot to open an investment account at the post office. I argued in favour of a new bicycle, but it was no good. He said I'd thank him when I grew up.

I forbore to point out that if I had many more close encounters with kidnappers, villainous foreigners and untrustworthy chauffeurs, I might not live to grow up. Parents should always be lulled into a sense of false security. Otherwise one gets no freedom at all.

5

The Case of the Red-headed Girl

After I had almost been bumped off by a group of blood-crazed kidnappers, my parents made me promise to try to keep out of trouble in future. I tried to explain that I never went looking for trouble. Instead, adventures seemed to seek me out. I pointed out that all the great heroes of the past, like Hercules and Robin Hood and so on, had had the same problem. My father was not impressed. He said you couldn't compare Hercules with a spotty twelve-year-old in spectacles and I was to 'watch it – or else'.

I agreed to make the effort and it was, in fact, almost a whole month before Fate once again decided to mess about with my life.

The whole thing began on a rather chilly day in October. Polly and I were on our way home from school, wheeling our bikes instead of riding them because we had matters of grave importance to discuss. We were always short of pocket money and we were debating whether or not to take on a paper round to improve our finances. Actually, the question was purely academic, as I was sure Polly's parents would never allow him to live so dangerously as to deliver papers and was pretty certain mine wouldn't either. Still, it does no harm to dream.

Suddenly Polly, who had been trying to calculate how much we could earn by Christmas, broke off to exclaim:

'Oh look, JB, I think that dog's following us.'

I turned round.

Behind us lolloped a huge St Bernard, which looked big enough to be on its way to audition for the Hound of the Baskervilles.

'It doesn't seem to have a cask of brandy with it, like on telly,' I said.

The creature caught us up. It stopped in a sociable sort of way and slavered hopefully, its tail wagging. I stretched out a hand. The tail-wagging redoubled in vigour. Tentatively I patted its head. The dog drooled at me in an ecstasy of delight. I looked at the name tag on its collar. It appeared to be called Bruno. Then I noticed something else.

'That's funny,' I said. 'It's got a bit of paper or something stuck in its collar.'

'Gosh!' said Polly. 'Now, in a serial on telly, that would be a message from a kidnap victim, asking whoever finds it to rescue them.'

'And in real life,' I said, 'it's probably a shopping list.'

I tugged hopefully at the paper. The dog, apparently under the impression that this was a new sort of game in which it was expected to join, cavorted unhelpfully round me. We waltzed together for a few minutes. Then I got the paper.

With difficulty, I unfolded the screwed-up missive and gazed at it unbelievingly. It read:

'I HAVE BEEN KIDNAPPED. I AM IMPRISONED IN THE ATTIC OF 40 BARTHOLOMEW AVENUE. PLEASE HELP ME.'

In silence I passed the note across to Polly, who read it slowly and then made his usual stirring contribution to the conversation.

'Gosh!' he said. 'What are we going to do, JB?'

I sighed.

'Go and see what makes at 40 Bartholomew Avenue, I suppose. Where is it, by the way?'

'Out on the very posh side of town.' Polly was definite on this point. I often reckon he knows the name of every road, avenue and back alley in the neighbourhood. Poring over street maps is one of his weird hobbies.

'So how do we get there?' I asked.

Polly thought for a moment.

'We turn right at the post office,' he said, 'then left at the roundabout. After that, I'm not sure. We'll have to ask.'

I withered him with a look.

'You can't ask the way when you're rescuing someone from kidnappers, you moron. Oh well, come on.'

We mounted our bikes. Bruno started an enthusiastic barking and galloped along the pavement beside us.

'Perhaps the dog's going to guide us,' Polly suggested.

'Then I wish he'd do it quietly,' I said irritably. 'If he's going to make that row all the way, we might as well arrive with a brass band. We lose the element of surprise.'

'Don't you think, JB,' my friend proposed hesitantly, 'that it might be better just to take the note to the nearest police station?'

'No, I don't,' I said. 'If it's not for real, we'll only

70

look silly. Like when we saw that girl murdered on Sark. Let's go and case the joint first.'

'You're the boss, JB.' Polly pedalled on trustingly.

After we had turned left at the roundabout, it simply became a matter of following the dog, who lob-lollied happily along, turning its head every so often to make sure we weren't getting left behind. It had, I was happy to note, no breath left to bark.

I wasn't surprised Polly hadn't been sure of the way after the roundabout. We turned right and left and right so many times that I began to wonder if, without the services of Bruno on the way back, we would ever reach home again. At last, however, we turned into a quiet, pleasant, tree-lined road, at the corner of which a name plate announced: 'Bartholomew Avenue'. Polly saw it too. He pointed it out in case I'd missed it.

'Look, JB!'

'I have,' I said shortly. 'Now we look out for number forty.'

Number forty was about halfway along the avenue on the right. Polly, seeing it, was about to dismount, when I hissed at him:

'Cycle past, you prat! Don't you ever watch thrillers on telly?'

'Sorry, JB.' Polly looked suitably abashed. We rode past, trying to look nonchalant and uninterested. A little way beyond the house a small road called Acacia Close opened off on the left. I signalled to Polly. We rode into the close, dismounted and parked our bikes against a garden wall. Polly was about to go through his usually lengthy performance with padlock and chain, when he saw the expression on my face.

'What's wrong, JB?'

'You are,' I said. 'Don't lock the thing. We may need to make a quick getaway.'

'Oh, sorry,' Polly apologized again. 'I'm just not used to this sort of caper. What do we do now?'

'We walk back,' I said, 'and stroll past the house.'

We did so. Bruno, slobbering happily, accompanied us.

As we ambled along Bartholomew Avenue, I began to cast furtive glances at number forty. My doubts about the escapade increased. It didn't look at all the sort of house in which kidnap victims were imprisoned. At least, not if all those telly serials were accurate, it didn't. It was a large modern detached house, standing well back from the road and surrounded by a garden so neat it put ours at home to shame. There was a wide gravelled drive with no suspicion of weeds in it and a huge double garage, which had a large room built over the top of it. Probably, I thought, the comfortable pad of the owners' chauffeur. I mean, it looked that sort of house.

Polly voiced my doubts almost immediately.

'Hey, JB, the note said: "imprisoned in the attic". That place hasn't got an attic. Perhaps it's the wrong house.'

'The dog doesn't think so,' I said. 'Look at him.'

Bruno, reaching a gallop at the thought of home and bickies, was racing up the drive and round the back of the house. A joyous bark, quickly fading, appeared to indicate that he had been let in.

'It's a hoax,' said Polly. 'We've been had. That dog's a practical joker.'

72

'Hang on,' I said. 'Look up at that window. There, over the garage.'

Polly looked.

A girl's face had appeared at the window of what I'd designated the chauffeur's pad. A pale face, surmounted by a mop of red hair. The face's nose was flattened against the glass. As we looked, a hand beckoned.

'Gosh!' said Polly blankly.

As a remark it didn't get us anywhere. We continued to gape. My usual quick reactions seemed temporarily frozen – probably with shock. The hand gestured again.

'I think,' said Polly carefully, 'she wants us to go round the back.'

'Come on then,' I said.

Polly hesitated.

'D'you think we ought? It's trespassing. They can send for the police.'

I glowered at him.

'Send for the police? When they've got her locked up there? You saw the note. She's been kidnapped. Come on.'

Polly still looked doubtful, but, like a good lieutenant, he followed me meekly up the drive. I kept one careful eye on the house. No doors opened. No curtains twitched. All was still. The occupant – or occupants – must be busy feeding Bruno in the kitchen, I thought hopefully. We trotted round to the back of the garage.

Once there, I breathed more freely. The back of the garage was not overlooked by any windows in the house. Unless they actually had armed guards lurking in the shrubbery, we were temporarily safe from observation.

The room over the garage obviously ran the full length of it, because the girl's face was now pressed against a window at the back. Behind the garage was a low shed, its flat roof almost on a level with the window. The girl beckoned again.

'She wants us to climb up,' Polly translated helpfully.

It was obvious that this was what the girl did want. I looked around. An apple tree formed an easy and tempting access to the shed roof.

I made one of my usual lightning decisions.

'I'm going up,' I announced. 'You stay on guard here. If you see anyone coming, hoot like an owl.'

'I can't,' said Polly flatly.

This is the sort of thing that tends to happen with Polly. In books I've read, people often signal danger to each other by hooting like owls. There never seems to be any sort of difficulty about it. Real life – particularly with Polly – appears to be quite different.

I sighed.

'Well, sing "God Save the Queen" or something. I'm off.'

I began my climb. I'd almost reached the roof when it struck me that Polly might look pretty odd standing in a stranger's garden singing the national anthem in his rapidly breaking voice. But it was too late now to start worrying about trifles.

I hauled myself on to the roof.

As I did so, the girl opened the window and leaned out. My doubts about the whole thing suddenly resurrected themselves. Really, they must be the most inefficient kidnappers to leave their victim with such an easy and tempting method of escape. Perhaps she was chained up to something. I approached the window and gazed in.

She wasn't chained.

Nevertheless, her first words bore out all the usual telly dialogue for such situations.

'You got my note,' she said. 'You've come to rescue me.'

'Well – er – yes,' I said.

I looked at her. She was about ten years old, small and pale and with this shock of red hair. She was wearing faded blue jeans, a rather grubby white sweater and sneakers. Then my eyes took in the scene behind her. It struck me that her kidnappers must be pretty kind-hearted. They appeared to have imprisoned her in a sort of playroom, which even contained a large rocking horse.

My doubts revived.

'Have you really been kidnapped?' I asked.

'Oh, yes. Well, in a way.'

'What sort of way?'

'It's my father. He and Mummy are divorced. I live with Mummy. But Daddy stole me when I was coming out of school yesterday. He's going to take me abroad with him. He's an American millionaire, you see.'

More kidnappers! I thought. Really, I seemed to have the same effect on kidnappers as a magnet has on iron filings.

Still, the story did now make more sense. In fact, I recalled seeing one very like it on telly only the previous week. Suddenly, however, my agile mind fastened on yet another snag.

75

'What about the dog?' I said suspiciously.

'What about him?' The girl sounded impatient. As well she might if she were indeed a kidnappee awaiting rescue.

'If he's your dog,' I said slowly, 'how come he's living here when you don't? And if he isn't your dog, how come you managed the note in his collar?'

The girl sighed.

'He *was* my dog,' she said. 'When the divorce came, Daddy took him. Please stop talking and take me away from here. Daddy's servants might kill you if they catch us.'

This decided me. I'd already had one unpleasant experience with overhasty kidnappers.

'Come on then,' I said.

The girl climbed out of the window. From below, Polly watched anxiously.

Another thought struck me. I stopped.

'What is it now?' asked the girl impatiently.

'How come you didn't just climb out and escape? It's easy enough.'

The girl looked me straight in the eyes.

'I've no head for heights. Are you going to help me, or stand talking till they catch us?'

I swallowed my doubts.

'Come on,' I said. 'I'll help you. Don't look down.'

A minute or two later we reached the ground. The girl had managed the climb with remarkable ease. Polly eyed us with disapproval.

'Is this wise, JB?'

'We've done it now,' I said. 'Come on.'

We crept cautiously round to the front of the garage. The house remained silent. No one seemed to be about.

'Run for it!' I said.

We all belted down the drive and out through the open gates. I seized the girl by the arm.

'This way.'

We raced down the road and turned, panting, into Acacia Close. Our bikes stood waiting for us.

'Can you ride a crossbar?' I said.

'Of course.' The girl sounded surprised.

'Get on, then.'

We mounted and pedalled furiously out of the close and away, not bothering, for the moment, about direction. I was just keen on putting as much distance as possible between me and any bloodthirsty kidnappers who might be in pursuit.

I must say I felt a proper Charlie with this kid on my crossbar. We'd been reading a soppy poem in school the week before about this daft guy, called Lochinvar or some such, who stole his girlfriend away just when she was on the point of being married off to another bloke. He swung her up on his horse in front of him and galloped off. The poem made the whole thing seem terribly simple. It never mentioned anything, for instance, about his having any sort of difficulty with her *hair*. This kid's hair, as well as being red, was quite long, and, with the speed we were going, it was blowing out behind her. I kept getting a mouthful of the stuff. In addition to which it was half blinding me.

I said irritably: 'Can't you do anything about your hair? It's getting in my way. I can't see the road.'

The girl laughed happily.

'I've lost my ribbon. Isn't this fun?'

I grunted. To me, it was appearing rather less funny by the minute, and I could see from Polly's face that he felt the same. Also, I was becoming hopelessly lost. I made another of my lightning decisions.

'Hang on,' I said, bringing my bike to a halt. 'We're far enough from the house now. Time for a council of war.'

Polly braked to a halt beside me. We both stood astride our bikes, eyeing the girl, who had dismounted and was pulling her socks up over her jeans.

'First,' I said, 'what's your name?'

'Miranda,' said the girl promptly. 'What's yours?'

'Never mind that for the moment,' I said hastily, cringing from the usual long explanation or misunderstanding my name always provoked. 'Now – we'd better take you to the nearest police station.'

Miranda looked alarmed.

'Oh no, not the police. Mother would be so upset. And besides, they might take me back to Father. He's very powerful in his own country, you know. They'd believe him rather than you.'

I hesitated. It was true that adults always tended to believe other adults rather than me.

'I say, JB, couldn't we just take her back to her mother?' Polly said tentatively.

'Good thinking,' I said. 'We'll do that. Where d'you live, Miranda?'

There was a long pause. Miranda just looked at me.

'You must *know*,' I said.

Really, girls are the *end*!

'Of course I know.' Miranda sounded indignant. 'It's just that –'

'Just what?'

'Well, it's a long way to go tonight. Especially on bikes.'

78

'Where is it?' I said.

'Dublin,' said Miranda.

There was an awkward pause.

Polly broke it. 'What shall we do, JB?' he asked. 'Mum doesn't like me to be late home.'

I frowned.

'She'll have to come home with one of us, I suppose. We'll sort it out in the morning.'

'She can't come home with me.' Polly was quite definite on this point. 'My parents would have heart attacks.'

I didn't see my parents being overjoyed either, if I arrived home with a penniless kidnap victim from Dublin. However, as number one man, it was up to me to take some action. Besides, we were already late and it was getting pretty dark. My own parents would be becoming edgy, while Polly's were probably having screaming fits by this time. I came to a decision.

'I'll take her,' I said. 'I can hide her in our Susan's room. Then, in the morning, we'll see.'

In my own mind I meant, 'In the morning I'll ring the police,' but I didn't say it out loud.

Polly had no such inhibitions.

'Let's go to the police now. It's easier.'

Miranda began to cry.

'Now look what you've done,' I said. 'No. We'll follow my plan. We must get home or the police'll be out looking for *us*.'

Polly, with thoughts of his mum uppermost in his mind, capitulated. Miranda brightened up. We remounted, with her perched once more on my crossbar, and rode off.

'Isn't this fun?' she said again.

Neither of us answered.

In point of fact, that journey home was a nightmare. Without the help of the faithful Bruno we kept getting lost and having to ask, but eventually we arrived back at the roundabout, after which Polly proved an efficient guide. He was by now a bundle of nerves, however, and kept consulting his digital watch every two minutes and rabbiting on about being late. After what seemed hours, we arrived at the corner where he always leaves me and turns into Laurel Grove.

'Good luck!' he said as he rode off. In the light of a streetlamp I caught a quick glimpse of his parents leaning anxiously over the gate; then I pedalled on with my burden.

It was after six o'clock when I arrived home. I dropped Miranda at the corner and told her to wait there till I had chance to smuggle her in. She wasn't too keen really, because it was beginning to rain, but I said if she didn't co-operate I'd go straight to the police. She gave in after that, and sort of melted into the shadows while I went on alone. It was a good job I did, because my dad was just getting the car out of the garage and swearing in a vicious, muttering sort of way. He glared when he saw me.

'Where d'you think you've been? I was just coming to look for you.'

'I – er – had a puncture,' I said.

My father looked at me suspiciously. I looked back with the open, honest sort of expression I keep for such occasions. He gave in.

When I got inside, my mother was in the hall, telephoning. As soon as she saw me she said, 'Oh, he's here now. I'll ring back,' and put the phone down.

'James, wherever *have* you been?' she demanded. 'I've been worried sick. I thought you'd been kidnapped.'

I couldn't help jumping slightly at the word 'kidnapped', but I offered the excuse about the puncture again. My mother seemed so relieved to see me home, and in one piece, that she didn't bother too much. Besides, by this time my father had put the car away and come in for tea, and, in the consequent bustle, my explanation was accepted.

I said: 'I'll just go and wash my hands,' and shot off upstairs.

I left the water running noisily in the bathroom and crept to the top of the stairs. My parents had both gone into the dining room and shut the door. I heard the television go on, so I crept back to turn off the tap. The TV would take all their attention. Then I snaked silently downstairs, quietly opened the front door and shot off down the path and along the road to the corner, where Miranda stood, trying to shelter from the rain under an inadequate laburnum.

'You took your time,' she snapped, as soon as she saw me.

'I came as quick as I could,' I said. 'It's not easy, you know – this sort of thing. Now, follow me, and once we get into the house don't make a sound.'

Miranda sniffed. But she followed me willingly enough, and, once we entered the hall, she waited while I soundlessly closed the front door, and then crept after me up the stairs. In fact, she appeared to be dramatizing the whole thing, tiptoeing along in exaggerated fashion and peering over her shoulder like a hunted animal. In silence we reached Susan's bedroom. I opened the door and we sneaked in.

81

'Now,' I whispered, 'you'll be safe here. But you must keep quiet.'

'I'm hungry,' said Miranda.

'OK, OK,' I said irritably. 'Give me time. I'll smuggle some food up to you later.'

Miranda eyed me balefully.

'Don't be long. I'm starving.'

My mother's voice floated faintly up the stairs.

'James, what are you *doing*? Your meal's getting cold.'

'Just coming,' I shouted.

With one final, anxious glance at Miranda, I slipped out, closing the door behind me. I wished I could have locked it but the key was missing. I set off downstairs.

My parents were watching the news on telly while they ate – a sure recipe for indigestion. I slipped into my chair, noting that it was steak and kidney pie, one of my favourites. I couldn't really enjoy it though. My mind was too preoccupied with how I was going to smuggle food up to Miranda. This is another thing that characters in books seem to have no difficulty with at all. In real life, the problem seemed almost insurmountable. I could hardly rise from the table and trot off upstairs with a plateful of pie. Such an action would be bound to invite comment. I decided that a better opportunity might come after the meal, when my parents were glued either to the telly or the evening paper.

Miranda would just have to wait.

The news dragged gloomily on towards its end. My father had just said: 'We'll hear the weather forecast, then I'll switch off,' when the newscaster suddenly announced:

'News is just coming in of a child missing from her home. Ten-year-old Miranda Biggins disappeared from her home at 40 Bartholomew Avenue shortly after four o'clock this afternoon.'

I paused with a forkful of pie halfway to my lips and began to listen in a sort of stunned horror.

The newscaster continued: 'Miranda had gone up to her playroom this afternoon after school. When her mother went to tell her that tea was ready, she found the room empty and one of the windows wide open. Miranda's parents, Mr and Mrs Biggins, ask that anyone with any idea of the child's whereabouts should inform the police immediately. Police are already questioning people living in the area. The number to ring is. . . .'

I watched the newscaster's lips in awful fascination. I was realizing that 'Biggins' didn't sound in the slightest like a swanky American millionaire's name, when the screen was suddenly taken over with a close-up picture of Miranda, while the newscaster described her – red hair and all. Accurate in every rotten detail, that description was!

I recalled all the various people from whom we'd asked directions on our way back to civilization, and my heart plummeted into my track shoes. Worst of all was the knowledge that I'd been had for a sucker. Taken for a ride. Me, James Bond, criminologist. And by a bit of a kid. A girl kid at that. And what, I asked myself bitterly, did James Bond do now, with the police from all over England yapping at his heels?

The picture of Miranda continued to leer out from the screen.

'Poor little thing!' my mother said. 'I wonder where she is?'

I made up my mind.

'Actually,' I said loudly, 'she's upstairs in Sue's room.'

Apart from the chattering of the TV, there was a sudden dead silence. My parents stared at me blankly. I stared back.

Stalemate.

There was the sound of running feet on the stairs. The door flew open. Miranda wasn't in Sue's room any longer. She was right with us.

'You rotten worm!' she said. 'You left me starving up there.'

We all three sat staring at her, unable to move. We might have been auditioning to become new exhibits at Madame Tussaud's.

My father was the first to regain his wits. He crossed to the television and switched it off. The weatherman was just forecasting storms. How right he was, I thought.

By this time Miranda had seated herself at the table. She beamed at my bewildered mother.

'That pie smells fab. Could I have some, please?'

As if in a daze, my mother ladled a helping of pie on to a plate and passed it to Miranda, who began to tuck in greedily.

My father, wearing the expression that never fails to quell me, said: 'Is your name Miranda Biggins?'

Miranda remained unquelled. She merely nodded, while continuing to gobble steak and kidney pie as if she had been starved for days. My father acknowledged defeat. He turned to me.

'What do you know about this, James?'

I took a deep breath.

'Well, it was like this. Polly and I were coming

84

home from school when we noticed this whopping great dog following us. It had a note in its collar saying someone had been kidnapped and was a prisoner at this house, see? So we went there. And we found her – ' I gestured towards Miranda – 'in a room over the garage. She said her father, who was a millionaire, had stolen her from her mother and was going to take her back to America. So we – er – rescued her, like – and. . . .'

My voice trailed away faintly under my father's unblinking stare.

'I don't believe a word of it, James. What have you been up to?'

'It's true,' I said. 'Look, here's the note.'

I fished out the crumpled letter from my pocket. My father read it and snorted in disbelief.

'James, you're an idiot,' he said.

Having thus summarily disposed of me, he turned to Miranda.

'I am going to ring your parents to tell them you're safe. What is your phone number?'

Miranda told him – indistinctly through a mouthful of pie.

Grimly my father went out to the phone in the hall.

My mother said, 'Oh, James, why can't you keep out of trouble?'

I shrugged wearily. Miranda finished the pie and began on the chocolate gateau. We were all trying to listen to the phone conversation. Also, I was beginning to wonder about Polly. If he'd seen the news item about Miranda, I tried to think what his reaction would be. Would he be desperately trying to contact me, or would his nerve have gone and caused him to confess to his parents?

Eventually my father returned.

'Miranda, your parents are coming straight over,' he said. 'And you, James' – he swung round on me – 'had better be thinking how you are going to apologize to them for your stupid actions.'

'It wasn't my fault,' I protested. 'You can't just ignore appeals for help, you know.'

'Could I have another piece of cake, please?' asked Miranda. 'It's jolly good.'

She continued to eat placidly.

The tense atmosphere was suddenly broken by a ring at the door bell, so loud and prolonged that it seemed as if someone were leaning on it. We all jumped.

'They've been quick,' said my father, and went to answer the door.

It wasn't the Biggins family, however. It was Polly with his mother and father. As soon as I saw the expression on his face, I knew that he'd broken under interrogation.

He just said: 'I'm sorry, JB.'

It was all he had time for, actually, before his mother let fly with her usual moan about how I always got her son into trouble and so on. Eventually, they were persuaded to sit down and calm down. Mum offered them both sherry, then she turned to me.

'I expect, James,' she said, 'that Paul's parents would like to hear your side of the story.'

'Well,' I said, 'it was like this. . . .'

I went through the whole saga again, though I felt that Mrs Perkins, at least, couldn't have cared less about my side of the story. I was just coming to the end of my account when the doorbell rang again.

This time it was Mr and Mrs Biggins.

I eyed them with interest. They really looked far too sensible to have a child as batty as Miranda – but then, you never know. Parenthood is an awful gamble.

Mr Biggins was tall and fair, while his wife was small and with red hair just like Miranda's – only much tidier. They assured themselves that their daughter was still in one piece, then they, too, were given drinks and settled down. My unfortunate name seemed to amuse Mr Biggins – who looked as if he might be a Fleming addict – but it was so obvious that the other oldies couldn't see the joke, that he quickly became serious again.

'Perhaps, James,' he said, 'you'd tell us exactly what happened?'

'Well,' I began wearily, 'it was like this. . . .'

At the end of my recital, Mr Biggins flung back his head and roared with laughter. After a bit, his wife joined in. No one else seemed to think it very funny.

'I'm so glad,' he said at last, wiping his eyes, 'that someone else has a child that gets into odd scrapes.'

My father looked at him like a drowning man reaching out for a trained lifeguard.

'You, too?'

'Rather,' said Mr Biggins enthusiastically. 'I remember when. . . .'

The next half-hour was spent with my parents swapping stories with Miranda's about our exploits. Personally, I didn't see any comparison. She did the daftest things. I could see Polly's mum deciding that this was yet another child who might be a possible danger to her son.

However, the evening passed rather more pleasantly

than I had feared. Mr Biggins' good humour seemed to affect all the oldies and I began to hope reprisals might be minimal.

They were. After all our guests had departed, my mother merely said:

'I hope you have learned a lesson from this unfortunate episode, James.'

'Oh, I have,' I said.

'What has it taught you, may I ask?'

'To keep away from girls,' I said. 'Girls are the *pits*!'

6
Polly and the
Lost Umbrella

Our half-term holiday fell at the very end of October.
The weather, knowing it was school holidays, did its
rotten worst to us, as if deliberately. It was cold, wet,
dreary and miserable. In addition to which, we had a
holiday task.

This was a local history thing. The idea was that
we should try to find out all about our area to way
back, by asking local oldies, finding old books,
photographing old buildings and a lot of nonsense of
that sort. Then we had to make a folder with all this
useless information written out neatly. It was
obviously going to take hours. Both Polly and I,
along with every other right-thinking boy in the form,
bitterly resented a holiday task. We regarded it as a
needless imposition. As Fatso Austin frequently
remarked, if our teachers couldn't impart all the
knowledge we needed during term time, they weren't
earning their money.

It was this despised holiday task, however, which
led to one of my most unusual and dangerous
adventures.

The affair began innocently enough. I had gone
round to Polly's house on the Wednesday evening to
help him test his new computer game. We'd spent an
enjoyable hour with the thing, when Polly returned

to the subject of the holiday task – which neither of us had done anything about.

'If we were to go into Camcaster tomorrow,' he suggested, 'we could look it up in the big reference library. I bet we could just copy whole chunks out of books there. Sir'd never know we hadn't been round doing all the research ourselves.'

'That's not a bad idea,' I said thoughtfully. 'Shall we go on our bikes in the morning?'

'All the way to Camcaster? On our bikes? In this weather?' Polly was horrified. 'My parents would start frothing at the mouth at the thought of it. We'll have to get the bus.'

'OK,' I said agreeably. 'There's one at ten o'clock. I'll call for you at quarter to. Let's get some lunch in a snack bar and make a day of it.'

Polly thought this was a sound idea, and even his mum couldn't find much wrong with our spending several hours working in a library – though she looked as if she'd like to try. Moreover, Polly pointed out that it was school work, and she's always on at him to do well at school, so she capitulated.

Really, compared with Polly's mum, my parents seem almost reasonable.

Nine forty-five the next morning, therefore, saw me beating a cheerful tattoo on Polly's front door. It was opened by Polly's mum. She was smiling until she saw who it was, but then she promptly switched the smile off and glowered at me.

'Oh, hello, James,' she said, in her distant, who-is-this-alien sort of voice. 'Paul isn't quite ready.'

There was a long pause, then she added reluctantly:

'You'd better come in.'

She opened the door just wide enough for me to squeeze into the hall. I gave her one of my placating-type smiles and spent ages ostentatiously wiping my feet. But I could see it didn't impress her.

'Be careful in Camcaster, won't you, James?' she began. 'I've already warned Paul. You know the Prime Minister's visiting that new computer factory today, don't you? So the town will probably be packed with undesirable people.'

She didn't make it clear whether or not she considered the Prime Minister an undesirable person. I don't believe in getting involved in politics – which I find dead boring anyway – so I kept tactfully silent. Actually, my father had already suggested that we might be lucky enough to see the Prime Minister. If, he had added bitterly, we managed to keep our eyes open for once.

Considering all the adventures I had already had merely by keeping my eyes open, I thought this a bit unfair. But, as I've mentioned before, you can't argue with my father.

Mrs Perkins was still rabbiting on in a complaining sort of way about being careful, when Polly came rushing down the stairs, apologizing for being late. His mum then went into her, 'Got a clean hanky, dear?' routine, which poor old Polly obviously has to go through every time he leaves the house. It was all most embarrassing and I blushed for him.

'Here. You'd better take your father's umbrella,' she said finally. 'It's going to rain. The weatherman said so.'

She handed the squirming Polly one of those big old-fashioned black rolled umbrellas which you see businessmen carrying on telly adverts. Polly tried to protest but it was no good. Moreover, I could see we were going to miss the bus if we didn't get away sharpish, so I said:

'That's a good idea, Mrs Perkins. Come on, Polly.'

I bundled him out of the door and down the path. His mother was still yelling final instructions about taking care, and wearing his scarf, and not getting his feet wet and so on, until we were out of earshot.

We just reached the bus stop in time to fling ourselves on to the moving vehicle. I wondered what Polly's mum would have said had she seen her son forced to risk life and limb with such a gymnastic display because she'd made us late.

'Mum does go *on*!' Polly said apologetically.

'We all have our cross to bear,' I said.

He seemed to find this comforting.

Our bus journey was uneventful, except that, when we came to get off, Polly almost left his umbrella under the seat and was only saved from a fate worse than death at his mother's hands by the swift action of a little old lady, who restored it to him by flinging it after us from the moving bus. From Polly's reaction I wasn't *quite* sure if his forgetfulness hadn't been intentional.

When we entered the library, almost the first thing we saw was a large umbrella stand just inside the door. Obviously lots of people besides Polly's mum had been listening to the weather forecast, because there were loads of umbrellas already there. Polly thankfully shoved his in among the others. Then he said:

'Oh, look, JB. There's another umbrella just like mine.'

I looked. The lad was right.

'Are you sure you'll know your umbrella again?' I said. 'They look exactly the same.'

'Oh, yes,' said Polly airily. 'If I look carefully. Mine's got AMP carved on the handle. See?'

He displayed it.

'AMP?' I said blankly. 'Why?'

'My dad's initials. Arthur Maurice Perkins. See?'

'You kids stop mucking about with those umbrellas,' said a voice.

I looked round. A tall, scraggy, bespectacled woman had materialized by us. Obviously an over-suspicious library employee. I gave her my innocent stare, but she wasn't fooled. We moved away.

There weren't many people in the reference part of the library when we got there. The librarian in charge of that section proved to be a male version of the tall, scraggy, bespectacled type we had just left. He eyed us suspiciously.

'If you kids think you're going to fool about in here, you can just think again.'

Honestly, I don't know what it is about Polly and me which makes adults automatically think the worst.

'We have come in to do some research work,' I said with dignity. 'Have you any books on the history of this area?'

'What period?' he said.

'From the Romans on, I should think,' I said. 'It's very detailed research.'

He gave us a doubtful look but he found the books for us – four of them – and showed us where we could sit. He couldn't, however, resist one final crack.

'I've got my eye on you, and don't you forget it.'

I gave him one of my withering looks and ostentatiously opened my smart new leather briefcase. I had at last persuaded my father that carrying my books to school in an old canvas duffel bag was rather letting the family image down. My mother had agreed with me, so Dad, under protest, had forked out for a briefcase – a super one, actually. Proper leather and with two compartments and my initials on it. Real snazzy. I hoped the librarian was impressed.

He wasn't.

We settled down to work.

'There's heaps of useful stuff here,' Polly said. 'Which chunks shall we copy out, JB?'

I gave him a look of scorn.

'We mustn't both copy the same bits, you moron. Even Sir'd smell a rat.'

'Of course.' Polly was suitably abashed. 'I don't know what I'd do without you, JB. I don't really.'

Privately I tended to agree with him, but I didn't want to hurt his feelings by saying so. We bickered for a while about which wodges each should copy, then began to write busily.

The scraggy librarian, who had been pretending to busy himself with some books, from a vantage point where he could watch us surreptitiously, began to relax and get on with his proper work.

Time passed.

About midday I yawned, looked at my watch and remarked: 'I'm hungry. Let's go and get a beefburger or something.'

For once Polly disagreed with me.

'We've so near finished the lot, JB,' he said. 'Why

don't we press on for a bit? Then we don't need to come back after lunch.'

I brightened.

'That's a thought. We could go in the park and feed the ducks.'

We settled down again.

It was shortly after one o'clock when I flung my pen down, stretched my stiff fingers and looked at Polly.

'Finished!' I said triumphantly. 'How're you doing?'

'On the last line.'

Polly, his tongue sticking out to denote earnest endeavour, scribbled on for a minute, then began to put his papers together. He had been using two fibre-tipped pens, so that he could put most sentences in black, but one or two in red. He appeared to have used both colours to scribble on his face and hands at odd intervals as well and now rather resembled a Red Indian warrior in full war paint.

'You've got ink all over your face,' I told him. 'We'd better wash.'

By the time we had handed in our books to the now friendly librarian and cleaned Polly up, it was about half past one and we were ravenous. As we arrived at the revolving doors leading to the world outside, Polly said:

'Oh, look! It's raining.'

That statement did the weather injustice. It wasn't just raining. It was bucketing down. I gazed out in dismay.

'Good job I've got that umbrella,' said Polly cheerfully. 'It's big enough for two.'

He went across to the umbrella stand and rummaged about a bit. Then he turned round to me.

'It's gone.'

'What has?' I said.

'My umbrella. It's gone.'

'It can't have.' I crossed to him. 'Look, idiot, there it is.'

'That's not m-mine.' Polly was beginning to betray signs of panic as usual. I think it's something he's inherited from his mum. 'That's the other one like it. I told you – m-mine has my dad's initials on.'

I yanked the umbrella out of the stand and examined it.

No initials.

I knew what Polly's next remark would be. Sure enough, he made it.

'What shall we do, JB?'

After a moment's thought I picked up the offending umbrella and strode across to the scraggy librarian (female version, Mark 1).

'Excuse me,' I said, using my highest quality of smarm, 'but someone seems to have taken my friend's umbrella. It was exactly like this, but with his initials on the handle.'

'Oh dear,' said the librarian helplessly.

She looked at the umbrella and thought for a moment.

'I remember,' she said triumphantly. 'It was a gentleman who left about half an hour ago. He took an umbrella the image of that one from the stand and rushed out with it. He seemed in quite a hurry. I expect that's how he came to make the mistake.'

She beamed at us in a self-satisfied sort of way as if the problem was now satisfactorily solved.

'But what are we to do?' I said. 'It's pelting down outside.'

'Oh dear!' said the librarian again.

We waited patiently while she put her ageing mind to this new puzzle.

'You'd better take that one,' she said at last. 'Then bring it back with you when next you come in. Probably the gentleman will have realized his mistake by then and returned *your* umbrella. Then we can sort out the whole thing.'

'My mum isn't going to like it,' Polly said.

'Oh, bother your mum,' I said. 'It's pouring, and I'm dying of hunger. Come on.'

So, with the librarian's blessing, we stole the alien umbrella and whirled our way through the revolving doors, going round several times for luck.

Once outside, Polly started to struggle with the catch of the umbrella, which seemed unusually stiff.

'Oh, come on, do,' I said. 'I'm getting soaked.'

'S-sorry, JB.' Polly was getting het up again. 'But it doesn't come open like Dad's d-does. There's sort of different controls on it.'

He made it sound like Concorde.

'Well, buck up,' I said. 'If I get much wetter I'll need a lifebelt not an umbrella.'

'Hang on,' said Polly agitatedly, swinging the umbrella downwards. 'There's a red button here. P'raps if I press that. . . .'

He pressed it.

There was a sort of plop sound and something whistled past me. My briefcase was suddenly torn out of my hand.

'That's funny!' said Polly.

'What happened?' I asked.

I bent to pick up my briefcase. Then I gasped. There was a small, neat hole right through it. I

97

looked at it blankly, holding the briefcase out in front of me to observe it better.

'The thing's not opening at all,' said Polly. 'It's just kind of spitting.'

He jammed his finger on the red button again. The plop was repeated. Something whammed into my briefcase again, almost wrenching it from my grasp. Another small, neat hole joined the first one in the brown leather.

The incredible truth suddenly dawned on me.

'You've shot my briefcase,' I said in astonishment.

'What?' Polly was still struggling with the umbrella.

'Don't do that,' I said, grasping his arm. 'Don't *touch* that umbrella. Look!'

I thrust my wounded briefcase under his nose.

After a long examination:

'I say!' he said in awe. 'Did I do that?'

'The umbrella did.' My agile mind was racing. 'It's a disguised gun. The owner must be a hit man like you see in American films.'

'I say!' repeated Polly, once again displaying his usual limited vocabulary. 'What shall we –'

'Find a policeman,' I said firmly, 'and explain.'

'Best thing,' nodded Polly at once.

We set off.

It must have been a policemen's holiday or something. We trotted on for ages in the pouring rain, looking for either one of our boys in blue or a lamp of the same colour. At length we turned a corner and saw a soggy, uniformed figure walking leisurely towards us.

Polly gripped my arm.

'The fuzz!' he hissed.

'All right. All right,' I said irritably. 'There's no need to talk like that. We're not criminals, you know. Come on.'

We approached the policeman.

'Excuse me,' I said.

He stopped and gazed down at us.

'Lost, are you?' he said kindly.

'No, we're not,' I said. 'It's this umbrella. It's not ours, you see and –'

'Where did you get it?'

'In the library,' I said. 'We'd left our umbrella in the stand, but when we came out ours had gone but this was there. So she said to take it. So we did. And it shot my briefcase.'

The policeman frowned.

'Are you trying to be funny, lad?'

Really, if all the representatives of law and order are so slow on the uptake, I'm not surprised the crime rate's soaring.

'It's this red button, see?' I said patiently. 'We thought it would open the umbrella, but it doesn't. It fires bullets.'

The policeman gave me a pitying smile and took the umbrella from my damp grasp. He examined it, pointing it skyward.

'Don't press that button,' I said warningly.

Too late. The constable already had.

There was the usual plop, then the sound of breaking glass as the street lamp above our heads shattered. We all jumped.

One or two passers-by turned their heads, but most just decided it was none of their business and hurried on.

'Blimey!' said the policeman blankly.

I gave him a few seconds to pull himself together. Then I uttered Polly's stock phrase.

'What d'you think we ought to do?'

The policeman was in no doubt about that.

'We'd best go along to the station,' he said. 'Sergeant'll know how to tackle this.'

I hoped, for all our sakes, that his touching faith was justified.

With the policeman gingerly bearing the umbrella as if it were a time bomb ticking away close to zero hour, we set off.

At the police station, the sergeant in whom our guide had such trust listened unbelievingly to our story and gazed even more unbelievingly at the umbrella. He appeared stunned. It wasn't until our constable described how he had murdered a lamp-post that the sergeant came to life.

'You did what?'

Stolidly the policeman repeated his account of the shooting. I displayed the remains of my briefcase as corroborative evidence. The sergeant took the umbrella and began to examine it.

'Don't touch the red button!' we all yelled like a demented Greek chorus.

The sergeant hastily lifted the finger which was almost upon the button. I was pleased to observe that his reactions were rather quicker than the constable's had been in similar circumstances. Then he said:

'Wait here. All of you.'

He disappeared into some mysterious regions beyond a green painted door. We waited for what seemed rather a long time.

'I'm ever so hungry,' Polly whispered.

'So am I,' I said. 'D'you suppose they'd give us something to eat if we asked?'

I spoke a bit loudly because a WPC was just passing and I thought a woman might prove more sympathetic to the needs of children.

She was. Having first ascertained from the constable that we were not juvenile delinquents awaiting retribution, she brought us two mugs of scalding tea and a cheese sandwich apiece. The tea was so strong that it could well have supported itself without the cup round it, but we were beyond caring. We were just polishing off this feast when the sergeant came back and asked us to accompany him. Dropping cheesy crumbs all over the floor, we obeyed.

We were taken through into a rather bare and dingy office, where a middle-aged man with a face like an intelligent whippet was sitting behind a desk. A younger, glamour type lounged in the window. We were offered chairs and then the middle-aged one said:

'Now, will you please tell us the whole story from the beginning?'

The beginning, of course, was really Polly's mum insisting on his taking the umbrella, but I knew he wouldn't want all that malarky, so I began where we arrived at the library and found the umbrella's twin awaiting us. Whippet-face listened without interrupting. Polly listened too, nodding agreement at intervals.

Finally Whippet Face said: 'So you never saw the man who took your umbrella?'

'Not a glimpse,' I said.

'The l-librarian did though,' said Polly suddenly.

101

'She saw him t-take the umbrella. She s-said he s-seemed in a hurry.'

Whippet Face nodded briefly at the sergeant, who faded through the door, presumably to third-degree the librarian on the phone.

I looked at the umbrella, now lying innocently on top of Whippet Face's desk as if it wouldn't dream of shooting anyone.

'Is that thing really a gun?' I said.

The man by the window spoke for the first time.

'It's far more than just a gun. That umbrella can fire bullets, take photographs, and send out and receive radio signals. It can even, at a push, be used to keep the rain off.'

'If you press the right button,' I said sourly, eyeing my briefcase.

Polly suddenly uttered again. Tentatively, but I could tell he was excited because he was still stammering.

'D-d'you think the man was g-going t-to use it to k-kill the Prime Minister?'

Oh, really, I thought. Poor old Polly! His parents really shouldn't let him watch so much telly. I waited for the guffaws.

But Whippet Face wasn't even smiling.

'We think it's a possibility,' he said. 'It's a good job you two boys were sensible enough to bring it straight to us. If we can get a description of the man from the librarian, we stand a very good chance of appre-hending him.'

I had a momentary vision of a hired assassin trying to murder the PM with an old umbrella belonging to Polly's dad. I didn't see what the police, in such circumstances, could charge him with. Though he'd probably finish up at a funny farm somewhere.

At that moment the phone on the desk started ringing.

Whippet Face answered it. It began to buzz away at him like a worried hornet, while he said, 'Yes, sir,' and 'No, of course not, sir,' at intervals. At last he said: 'Thank you, sir. I will,' and put the phone down.

Then he turned to us.

'I think you are entitled to know,' he said, 'that a known terrorist has just been arrested in the town. He was standing in the crowd by the factory steps as the PM went in. He appeared to be trying to open his umbrella.'

I voiced the doubt which had been troubling me.

'He hasn't actually *done* anything though, has he?'

Whippet Face smiled.

'The antiterrorist branch want him for other crimes, but, until today, he has managed to elude them. You two have helped considerably. What are your names, by the way?'

I cringed inwardly and hesitated. Polly had no such inhibitions.

'I'm Paul Perkins,' he said. 'And –'

'My name's James Bond,' I said defensively.

The young man by the window began to grin, but Whippet Face merely said, 'Very suitable too.'

My heart warmed to him.

By this time it was clear that Polly was obviously worrying about something. He fidgeted about and cleared his throat and dithered around a bit. At last he said:

103

'Will I ever get the umbrella back? It's my dad's, you see.'

Whippet Face smiled.

'It will be returned to you eventually, don't worry. For the moment it's evidence, I'm afraid.'

I could see Polly wasn't really happy about this, and, knowing how his mum goes on, I couldn't blame him. I had my own worry, too.

Consequently we were both rather silent going home in the bus.

'How on earth am I going to explain this to Dad?' I said at last.

I held up my briefcase with the two bullet holes drilled neatly through it.

'My dad paid the earth for this briefcase,' I said miserably. 'He'll never let me have another as long as I live. Whatever can I say to him?'

'Tell him the truth,' said Polly. 'After all, you've saved the PM's life, JB. You ought to be a national hero.'

I snorted.

'The truth? That you shot my briefcase with your umbrella? Don't be daft. He'd never believe me. And he'll be in such a tizz he won't even listen.'

'Oh, I don't know,' said Polly seriously. 'Remember George Washington.'

'Have you gone bonkers?' I said. 'What's George W. got to do with it?'

'When he'd chopped down that cherry tree, he told his dad the truth, and, because of that, his dad said right away that he forgave him.'

'True,' I said sardonically. 'But don't forget that lad had a hatchet in his hand at the time. I shan't be so lucky.'

I wasn't!

7

The Bonfire-night Burglar

When we returned to school after half-term, Polly and I were able to boast of how we'd saved the Prime Minister from assassination. At first, none of our classmates believed us, but when I displayed the holes drilled through my briefcase, I could see the doubters begin to waver. Even Fatso Austin, having examined my damaged case with a magnifying glass, was heard to mutter that some people had all the luck. While Fred Parkin, whose dad hates the PM, said I shouldn't have interfered in the course of justice. Naturally Polly and I exaggerated the story a bit, until finally the rumour got around that I'd actually flung my briefcase at the killer as he fired. Kids who'd already heard of my previous adventures began to eye me with almost superstitious awe. It was all highly satisfactory.

It looked as if I should be able to keep on displaying the briefcase for the rest of my school career, as my furious father had flatly refused to buy me another. It didn't bother me, except that when we had our habitual wet weather, my books got a bit soggy and some of the staff became rather tetchy about this. Finally, I started wrapping my homework in plastic bags before stowing it in the briefcase, which worked quite well. After this, I carried my spoils of war with pride and wouldn't have relinquished it even if a new one had been offered. Which it wasn't.

However, the other kids soon had something more exciting than my briefcase to take their attention. The Saturday following our return to school was the fifth of November and we all began to look forward to that. There was going to be a big bonfire, as usual, on the field next to the church hall. Everyone had been adding to it for weeks, and the vicar's wife had made us a really super guy. Quite lifelike he was, in an old gardening jacket of the vicar's, corduroy trousers donated by the verger and a scarf proclaiming that he supported Manchester United. The vicar's wife had given Polly and me a preview of him when we'd called at the vicarage with some jam my mum had made for the autumn fair, and that guy was really something.

The bonfire itself was to be lighted by the vicar in person – the Reverend John Smiley. Incidentally, I've never known anyone more aptly named than our vicar. He always wore an apologetic half-smile as a sort of extra vestment. In addition, he always seemed to be washing his hands with an invisible bar of soap. We were reading *David Copperfield* at school this term, and every time the character Uriah Heep was mentioned, I thought of the Rev. John Smiley. He would have been a natural for the part.

As we rode home from school on the Wednesday afternoon, Polly said:

'Have you asked yet about the bonfire?'

I should tell you that the only disadvantage each year with this bonfire is that no children are admitted to the field without an accompanying adult. Usually, all our parents draw short straws or something and the losers take two or three kids each. Last year Polly's dad had taken us. This year we had both assumed that my mum or dad would take over. But, up to now, they'd said nothing and we were getting worried.

'Not yet,' I said. 'I'll try tonight.'

'Mum isn't keen for me to go,' said Polly sadly. 'Not unless your parents'll take us.'

'What about your dad?' I said. 'He enjoyed it last year.'

'He's going to the Rotary Club dinner on Saturday, so he can't.'

'Well,' I said, 'my dad's not what you call a fun man, but I'll try.'

I made my request about the bonfire at what I considered the most strategic point of the evening – after my father had enjoyed his meal and before he got bedded down in front of the telly.

'Can't Paul's dad go?' he protested.

'It's the Rotary Club dinner,' I said.

'Well, I'm not going,' he said. 'I've got a meeting at the golf club which is likely to go on late.'

'And I'm certainly not going,' said my mother. 'I hate bonfires. Noisy, smelly things!'

Stalemate.

'It's your turn, Dad,' I said.

'Rubbish!' said my father.

'But who'll take us then?'

My father frowned.

'James, stop nattering on. You'll find someone. Ask around.'

'Most people have already got their quota,' I said.

'Then you'll have to give it a miss this year, won't you?'

'But –'

'That's enough, James,' snapped my father. 'Do your homework.'

I lapsed into a dignified silence.

'And don't sulk,' said my mother.

You can't win, can you?

I spent the next half-hour writing an essay and inventing wild schemes to get me to that bonfire. I needn't have bothered. The matter was resolved for me later in the evening when Auntie May arrived.

Auntie May is my mother's younger sister, and, as aunts go, she's not half bad. She's thin and wiry and athletic-looking. She had once played hockey for England, is quite competent at judo and is currently Akela for the local pack of Cubs. She solved the problem the moment I cunningly put it to her.

'Of course you mustn't miss the bonfire,' she said heartily. 'Now, I'll be there helping organize it, so I can keep an eye on the pair of you. It begins at seven. I'll collect you both at half-past six and tell the people at the gate you're with me. You'll have to get yourselves home though. I'll be staying to help the vicar clear up.'

'That OK, Dad?' I said.

'Fine,' said my father, looking relieved that Auntie May had got him off the hook.

My mother, however, wasn't satisfied.

'What time does the bonfire finish, May? I don't want them coming home late on their own.'

'Prompt at nine,' said Auntie May. 'There'll be some quite young children there, you know. Including my Cubs.'

'Oh, well, if it's no later. . . .' My mother was obviously weakening.

'Yippee!' I said. 'Ta, Auntie May. I'll just ring Polly and tell him.'

I shot off into the hall before Mum could change her mind again.

When I phoned Polly and told him the good news, I could hear him having difficulties with his mum at the other end of the line. Then I heard his father's voice say:

'Oh, don't mollycoddle the lad, Muriel. Let him go. May Hunt's a sensible woman. They'll come to no harm.'

So it was arranged, and we began to look forward to Saturday night with mounting excitement.

On Thursday evening two things happened, both of which seemed to have nothing to do with me at the time, but each, in its own way, was to affect me later.

First of all, my sister Susan rang up. She doesn't often ring us, unless she needs some more money, but this time it was a different request.

I took the call, because my mum was out and Dad was watching snooker on telly. He's a snooker *addict*.

'Oh, is that you, James?' Sue said. 'OK. Then listen carefully and *try* to get this right. I'll be coming home on Friday night for the weekend because Evelyn and I are going to Emma Harrington's birthday party on Saturday. It's going to be a rather super fancy-dress affair. Emma's driving us both up in her new car. Ask Dad to book a room at the Spotted Cow for Evelyn for two nights, will you? Have you got that?'

'Got it,' I said.

'Recap,' she ordered.

'You're coming home on Friday night,' I said obediently. 'Dad's to book a room for your drippy boyfriend at the Spotted Cow for Friday and Saturday. That all?'

As Sue was speaking from a call box which appeared to be gobbling ten-pence pieces like a hungry boa constrictor, she didn't rise to the bait about the 'drippy boyfriend'. She merely said crossly:

'That's all. Don't forget.'

'I never forget things,' I said. 'All my teachers say I've got a super memory.'

'Little creep!' she snapped. And rang off.

I conveyed her message to Dad.

'Has she still got that wet lettuce of a young man in tow?' he asked. 'OK. I'll ring the pub when the snooker's finished. Emma'll be twenty on Saturday, won't she? I bet her parents put on a good party. Sue should enjoy it.'

I agreed with him that it was likely to be a good party. The Harringtons hadn't just got money. They were wallowing in the stuff.

They lived in a large, posh house which was actually quite newish but spent its time trying very hard to look Georgian. It was called the Stone House, which I always thought was a bit silly as it wasn't stone at all but bright red brick. But I suppose 'Stone House' sounded more classy. Emma and our Sue were about the same age. They'd been through school together, had been best friends for years and had both started at the same university on the same day – though Emma was studying Eng. lit. Until the advent of Evelyn they'd gone everywhere together. Lately, we'd heard less of Emma, but obviously the friendship was still on.

The other thing that happened that Thursday night was that there was another break-in. There'd been several houses burgled in our area over the past months. Not houses like our hovel, of course. This bloke – or blokes – went only for the big stuff. He seemed to know who had valuable jewellery or vast amounts of money in the house on any given night. And he was a wizard with safes. Major Blount had had his burglar-proof safe rifled only a fortnight previously, while he and his wife snored happily in the room above. No mindless vandalism with this character. He nipped in and out of the house in silence, disturbing nothing, but quietly removing what he wanted. A real professional, the press said. They began to call him 'Raffles' and make gibes about the incompetence of the local police.

In fact, they made him sound so glamorous, I began to wonder if perhaps I wouldn't be a burglar when I grew up!

I first heard of the break-in on Friday morning. It was on the radio at eight o'clock. A character called Felix Mount, who lived the other side of Elwich, had had all his valuable collection of Georgian silver nicked. Same pattern as the other recent crimes, chattered the newsreader. Obviously the work of our friendly neighbourhood Raffles.

'Poor old Mount,' said my father, switching off the radio. 'He'll be devastated. He loved that silver.'

'D'you know him?' I asked idly.

'Met him at golf,' said my dad. 'Nice bloke. The Harringtons had better look out. I should think they're on Raffles' list.'

'P'raps he'll be at the party,' I said. Then, in the rush of gobbling my cornflakes, finishing my homework, collecting Polly and getting into school on time, I forgot the whole thing.

For the moment, that is.

I remembered it again at morning break though. Sharon Mills, in our class, has a dad who's a detective sergeant in the local force. Usually she doesn't talk about him much, because the fuzz aren't always too popular with some of our dimmer contemporaries, but this morning she was fairly bursting with pride.

'You've heard about the break-in at the Mounts, haven't you?' she asked. 'Well, my dad's been put in charge of the whole case. It'll mean promotion when he solves it.'

'*If* he solves it,' said Fatso Austin coldly. 'Your dad and his crowd haven't been very successful up to now, have they?'

'They will be now my dad's in charge,' protested Sharon.

We all jeered at that, so Sharon promptly ran back into school, pursued by her cronies, all yearning to be Florence Nightingales and comfort her.

Really, girls are so *wet*.

As we went into school at the end of break, Polly, who had been unusually silent and thoughtful for the past five minutes, said:

'Why don't *you* catch him, JB?'

'Catch who?' I said.

'This Raffles character.'

'How?'

'I don't know, JB,' said Polly humbly. 'I'm not very good at these things. But I'm sure you'll think of something.'

I thought about it all through history, with the

result that I absentmindedly told Sir that the First World War had been ended in 1918 by the signing of the Magna Carta. This earned me a detention, plus a spontaneous round of applause from the class.

After which, I dismissed the whole thing from my mind. The opportunity of catching Raffles wasn't likely to present itself to me, anyway. My parents imposed a strict nine-thirty curfew. Raffles was likely to be allowed out somewhat later.

Besides, there were more immediately exciting things to think about. Like bonfires, for example.

Prompt at seven o'clock on Friday evening, Emma Harrington's swish new car screeched to a halt outside our front gate and decanted Susan and her weekend case. My sister came rushing into the house announcing that she was just going to change before going straight out again, as Evelyn was treating both her and Emma to dinner at the Spotted Cow. My mother, who has got used, by this time, to catching just an occasional fleeting glimpse of her elder offspring, merely said placidly:

'Don't be too late home, dear.'

'Oh, I shan't,' said Sue. 'I've got to rig up my costume for tomorrow night when I get back.'

'Why don't you just hire a fancy dress from that shop in Camcaster?' asked my mother reasonably.

'It's against the rules, that's why,' retorted Sue. 'Everyone's got to concoct something for themselves without spending any money. There's going to be a prize for the most original costume. And you know the Harringtons always give *fabulous* prizes. I thought I'd go as a Dresden china shepherdess.'

I heard my father mutter 'Highly original,' from behind his newspaper, but Mum merely said: 'Very

113

nice, dear,' as Susan disappeared into her bedroom.

I'd been sent off to bed by the time she got back from the Spotted Cow, but I gathered from the conversation at breakfast next morning that the shepherdess idea had proved impracticable. Sue was getting very fraught about the whole thing.

'I've nothing to wear. Nothing,' she announced tragically. 'I can't go to Emma's party, that's all.'

'Why don't you go as a guy?' I said. 'It is the fifth of November, after all.'

'Don't be unkind, James,' said my mother.

But Susan's face lit up.

'James!' she screeched. 'What a brill idea! You've hit the jackpot for once. Dad, can I have that old tweed jacket of yours that was going to the church jumble? And I'll wear my old torn jeans and track shoes and –'

'It's not a very pretty costume, dear,' said my mother doubtfully.

Sue stared at her.

'Pretty? Who wants to look *pretty*? The prize is for originality.'

So it was settled. As far as our Sue went, my stock had never been higher.

Saturday seemed absolutely endless, but at last the evening arrived, and, promptly at half-past six, Auntie May's ageing Fiat drew up at our gate. I was already in the front porch waiting, but Polly, of course, having had mother trouble again, was late. He arrived, puffing and panting, just as I was scrambling into the car. I noticed he was carrying his wellies in one hand.

'What've you brought those for?' I said. 'It's not raining.'

'Mum thought the field might be wet. Can I leave them in your front porch, JB? I'll collect them on the way home.'

'Feel free,' I said generously.

Having dumped the wellies, we set off. Polly leaned back in his seat with a sigh of satisfaction.

'The adventure's begun, JB.'

'We're on our way,' I agreed.

We yipped a bit after that, until Auntie May told us to shut up, at least until she was out of ear-shot.

The bonfire was just terrific from beginning to end. The guy looked super and, when he caught fire, rockets shot from his pockets into the sky. The fireworks were fantastic. It was noisy and sparkling and breathtaking, and then, as the fire gradually began to die down and the last firework had exploded, some of the oldies began coming round with the eats. We stuffed ourselves with baked potatoes and parkin and crisps and roast chestnuts and pop, all mixed up in a scrumptious, yummy medley. The whole thing was fab.

At nine o'clock, Uriah Heep, using a megaphone, told us all to go home, except for the kind people who had offered to help him clear up. We gave him three cheers, at which he smiled even more than usual and washed his hands with redoubled vigour.

Auntie May materialized beside me.

'You two OK for off, now? Enjoy it, did you?'

'Thanks, Auntie May,' I said. 'It was fab.'

'Brill!' endorsed Polly. 'Thanks, Miss Hunt.'

'Right. Off you go now. Don't hang about or my name'll be mud. Scarper, there's good lads.'

We obediently scarpered.

'That was great!' said Polly with deep satisfaction, as we trotted swiftly along the moonlit street.

'Super-duper!' I agreed. 'Hey, look, there's the Harringtons' all lit up. Sounds a good party. You can hear it from here.'

'Sounds a drunken orgy,' said Polly primly.

He's very like his mum in some ways.

We paused by the Harringtons' gate to yearn and drool a bit, thinking about all that fab food inside. After a minute or two Polly said uneasily:

'Come on, JB. Mum said I wasn't to be late.'

'Hang on,' I hissed. 'Look!'

One of the French windows at the side of the Harringtons' house had opened. The room behind it was unlit, but, in the moonlight, we could clearly see a black-clad figure slip silently out on to the gravelled path, carefully closing the window behind it.

Polly gasped and clutched my arm tightly. I dragged him into the shadows by the gatepost.

As the figure turned we saw that not only was it dressed from head to foot in black, the face appeared to be black too, as it was covered completely by a sort of black hood with holes cut for the eyes. In one hand the figure carried a bulky sack.

After a swift glance round, the masked intruder began to run silently towards the Harringtons' double garage. He fumbled for a second with the catch. Then the door opened and the figure slid through it into the darkness within. Silently the door closed behind him.

'Gosh!' said Polly blankly. 'What was all that about?'

I looked at him in disdain.

'Don't you ever listen to the news? It must be

116

Raffles, of course. Dad said he'd be bound to try the Harringtons' sooner or later.'

'Gosh!' repeated Polly.

I waited for the inevitable follow-up. It came.

'What shall we do, JB?'

'We lock him in the garage,' I said promptly.

'Lock him in?' Polly's voice rose to a squeak. 'How?'

I glared at him.

'Don't make such a row, you moron. Most people leave the padlock hanging loose on the garage door, don't they? All we've got to do is creep over there and lock it.'

'He may be armed.' Polly was getting the willies again.

'Raffles doesn't use violence,' I said. 'The newspaper says so. Anyway, you stay here and keep cave. I'll go. It's dead easy.'

'Be careful, JB,' whispered Polly nervously.

I began to run silently across the drive as I'd seen the hero do in all those telly films. They never seem to have any difficulty about it. I didn't find it so easy. Just try running silently on gravel! I sounded like an overactive bowl of Rice Krispies when you pour the milk on.

I hoped the papers were right about Raffles never using violence. I also hoped he suffered from slight deafness.

I reached the garage.

They say fortune favours the brave. It does. The padlock was dangling loose from the hasp.

It was comparatively simple to lock it. It was not quite so simple to do it quietly. My heart was hammering so loudly that I was convinced it must be

117

audible for miles, and I seemed to have more than my usual quota of thumbs.

After a bit of fumbling I clicked the lock. As I did so, I noticed that a faint light was spilling out through the window at the side of the garage. It was too steady for a torch. Raffles must have switched on the light in the interior of one of the cars.

I crept back to Polly.

'JB, I've been thinking,' he said. 'What's Raffles doing in the garage?'

I gave him a pitying look.

'Stealing a car, of course. He's got the loot. You saw that sack he carried. Now he needs a getaway car. If I were Raffles I'd nick the Jag. It's the fastest.'

'Of course.' Polly's puzzled frown disappeared. 'You're always so quick on the uptake, JB. And the way you locked that garage! It was brill, mate. Just brill!'

'Piece of cake,' I said casually.

'What shall we do now, JB?' asked Polly.

I hadn't thought that far, actually.

'Go for the police, I suppose,' I said uncertainly.

Polly cleared his throat diffidently. I waited.

'It's quite a way, JB,' he said. 'He could break out. Why don't we just go up to the house and tell Mr Harrington?'

I think I've mentioned before that, although Polly is basically a bit thick compared to me, he does have these odd flashes of brilliance.

'Good thinking,' I said. 'Come on.'

We jogged up the drive to the front door and rang the bell.

It was answered by one of the Harringtons' au pair girls. They have two. One is large and blonde and

Swedish, the other small, dark and French. I was glad to see that it was the French one. She does speak a bit of English and understands quite a lot. The Scandinavian type is limited to 'Hello,' 'Goodbye,' and 'I not understand.'

'Could we see Mr Harrington, please?' I asked.

'He is at party.'

'I know,' I said patiently. 'This is important.'

'Matter of life and death,' added Polly helpfully.

This comment appeared to bewilder Mademoiselle – as well it might. However, she let us into the hall, carefully shutting the front door behind us.

'You wait, plis,' she said worriedly, and disappeared through a door at the end of the hall.

We waited.

'D'you suppose he'll be long?' asked Polly anxiously. 'My mum –'

Fortunately for the lad's peace of mind, he was interrupted by the arrival of Mr Harrington, who came bustling – as only a small, fat, self-important man can bustle – through the end door.

'What is all this?' he said irritably. And then, 'Oh, it's you, James. Nothing wrong at home, is there?'

'Not at home,' I said. 'Here. We've just caught a burglar making off with your family silver and stuff.'

'What!' Mr Harrington looked flabbergasted. 'Is this some sort of joke, James?'

'No joke,' I said. 'We saw him creeping out of the house –'

'With a big sack,' added Polly eagerly.

'So I locked him in your garage,' I finished.

'Did you indeed?' Mr Harrington appeared to have grasped the salient facts with commendable

119

speed for an oldie. 'Good show, James. We'll go get him. I'll just call out the posse.'

He darted off to the door from behind which all the row was coming and flung it open.

'Listen, all of you,' he bellowed above the din.

He was obviously used to command. An immediate silence fell.

'We've been burgled,' he continued, 'but these two bright lads here have trapped the thief in our garage. Who'll come and help me bring him in?'

Everyone in the room leapt forward eagerly.

'I'll take four.' Mr Harrington was beginning to sound like an army officer. 'You, Ted, and John, David and Jim. That'll be enough. Milly,' he turned to his wife, 'ring the police.'

'Yes, dear.' Mrs Harrington trotted off obediently.

Mr Harrington swung round on his heel and set off for the garage.

Despite his instructions, the whole crowd followed him. Including us. There was a lot of laughter and the odd shout of 'Yoicks!' and 'Tally-ho!'

We made our noisy way to the garage – alerting Raffles, I thought bitterly, every step of the rotten way.

As we crossed the drive, Guy Fawkes appeared at my elbow.

'Isn't this exciting?' said my sister's voice. 'Evelyn's missing all the fun though. I can't see him anywhere.'

Personally, I didn't think capturing burglars was really Evelyn's cup of tea. He may *look* like Superman, but there the resemblance ends.

We all arrived (noisily) at the garage.

Mr Harrington fished out a key from his pocket

and inserted it into the padlock. A sudden silence fell all around me, one of those breathless silences, while everyone waited for the climax. I almost expected the music to build up, like on telly.

Mr Harrington flung open the door of the garage and switched on the lights as he did so.

'Come out with your hands up,' he bellowed. 'I've got the place surrounded.'

It was nice to know I wasn't the only telly fan in the crowd.

Everyone pressed forward into the doorway and peered eagerly in. At first I thought the garage was empty, then I saw some movement inside the Jag.

Mr Harrington saw it too.

'Come out of that car,' he ordered. 'I can see you in there.'

From the back seat of the Jag two heads suddenly bobbed up, reminding me irresistibly of Punch and Judy.

Two heads?

'Out!' snapped Mr Harrington.

From the offside door a black-clad figure emerged. It was, however, no longer masked and I saw its face for the first time. A white, scared face it was too.

I gasped.

'Raffles' was Evelyn Smythe!

For a moment I thought my sister had been going around with a master criminal. A suburban gangster's moll, no less. However, it was only for a moment. From the nearside door appeared a girl, dressed as a scantily attired Greek maiden – ancient Greece, of course.

The girl was Emma Harrington.

In one of those blinding flashes they talk about, the

whole situation became clear to me. It obviously became equally clear to my sister. Sue let out a wail – whether of anguish or anger I wasn't sure – turned on her heel and rushed back to the house.

There was one of those tense pauses you read about.

Mr Harrington broke it.

'I see. Perhaps, before we catch pneumonia, we could all go back to the house. Emma, I'll talk to you later. Evelyn, I think you owe Susan an apology. Jim, run and tell my wife to cancel that call to the police.'

Evelyn, his face now deep crimson, began to mutter something indistinguishable. Amid muffled sniggers, everyone began to return to the house. The excitement was obviously over.

'I'm sorry, Mr Harrington,' I said. 'I'd forgotten it was a fancy-dress thing. We really thought it was a burglar.'

Mr Harrington surveyed the wretched Evelyn, who was still clutching his sack.

'That,' he said coldly, 'is hardly surprising. Look, would you two lads like to come in for a bit?'

I was on the point of accepting, because I could quite see that with Sue in her present mood, it was going to be my only chance of getting any of the gorgeous grub. Polly, however, had other ideas.

'Thanks, Mr Harrington,' he said, 'but we were supposed to be home for half nine.'

Mr Harrington glanced at his watch.

'In that case,' he said briskly, 'you're pretty late now. You'd better cut along sharpish.'

Polly scuttled off immediately. Reluctantly, I followed him.

We didn't talk much on the way home for the

122

simple reason that we met Polly's parents almost at once. They were hurrying down the road in search of the prodigal. Glowering viciously at me, they rushed off with their prize.

It was at that point I remembered that Polly's wellies were still standing to attention in our front porch. Fortunately his mother appeared too upset to notice their absence.

I completed the rest of my journey home at the gallop. It would be too shamemaking if my parents came out to look for me.

I made it, but only just. They were on the point of emerging from the front door, equipped with duffel coats and torches, as I panted up. I was dragged indoors for interrogation.

Fortunately, a distraction occurred almost at once, as Sue arrived, breathless and sobbing. She rushed off upstairs in a distraught sort of way. My mother followed her.

My father and I were left staring at each other.

'What was all that about?' he asked.

'I think,' I said anxiously, 'that I can explain.'

My father looked resigned.

'I might have known,' he said bitterly, 'that if there was any trouble, you'd be the cause. What have you been up to this time?'

'Trapping Raffles,' I said. 'At least, we thought it was, but it wasn't. It's why I'm late, really. You see, it was like this. . . .'

At the end of the story my father was silent for a long, thoughtful minute. Then he looked at me.

'James,' he said, 'do you think we've seen the last of Mr Smythe?'

'It looks like it,' I said. 'I'm sorry, Dad. But I really thought he was a burglar.'

I stood there uncomfortably, waiting for the storm to break.

My father said: 'Sue'll get over it. Off you go to bed now. You're very late. And, James –'

'Yes?' I said cautiously.

'Well done!' said my dad.

I blinked at him. He was grinning broadly. After a moment I turned and went slowly upstairs.

I'll never understand grown-ups!

8
The Third Man

After the 'Raffles' fiasco I determined to have nothing more to do with crime of any description. Armed robbers could invade the post office while I was queuing to buy a second-class stamp, old ladies could be mugged by villains under my very nose and drug peddlers could flog their wares openly in the High Street. I wasn't interested. I was keeping clear. I had no intention of making a fool of myself ever again.

Fortunately, the embarrassing story of the unmasking of Evelyn Smythe hadn't reached my mates at school. Polly, as usual, was loyal unto death, the Harringtons probably had their own reasons for keeping quiet about the episode, Sue had returned to her red-brick forcing house, and the other people at the party had all been in her age group and not likely to be interested in the doings of two whom they – quite wrongly – thought of as kids. After a week or so, when I'd heard nothing further of the humiliating episode, I began to breathe more freely.

However, my resolution remained firm. No more adventures for this James Bond. I confided my decision to Polly. He thought about it in silence for a minute or so – he never was a quick thinker – then he said:

'I don't think it'll work, JB. Some people are born to adventure. They can't avoid it. I think you're like that.'

'We'll see,' I said.

'And Raffles is still at large,' added Polly.

'Let him remain so,' I said generously.

'It would be a score though.' Polly sounded wistful. 'I mean, if we could catch him where the police have failed and –'

'I told you,' I said. 'I'm not interested.'

Polly gave me the sort of look a Saint Bernard dog might have given if, after a long trek through icy wastes, it had found the traveller already dead. But he said no more.

It was about this time that we began to notice some activity in the house next door to us – the one that formed the Siamese twin, as it were, to our semi. It had been up for sale ever since August, when the family living there, having produced yet another baby, moved to somewhere larger. Now, however, the 'FOR SALE' notice was replaced by a triumphant 'SOLD', and we realized that we were about to have new neighbours.

Mum promptly began to worry about what they would be like. She kept rabbiting on about the possibility of punk-style teenagers, screaming babies, yapping dogs and the like, while Dad hoped they would keep their garden tidy and maintain the right tone in the neighbourhood.

I've never quite understood what is meant by 'tone', but I'll tell you one thing – it's dead important in our street.

About a week later, when I arrived home from school one Friday evening with the prospect of a whole glorious weekend before me, I noticed that the 'SOLD' board had disappeared, curtains were beginning to appear at the windows and a large ginger cat was glaring out balefully through the glass of the sun porch.

Obviously we now had our new neighbours.

I put my bike in the shed and went in to tea. Mum was singing 'Climb Every Mountain' as she lifted a tray of scones out of the oven, so I knew everything was all right. If she's upset she changes to 'Nobody Knows the Trouble I See, Lord' until things calm down.

She greeted me with a wide smile.

'Our new neighbours have moved in,' she announced.

'Yeah,' I said. 'I noticed. Can I have one of those scones, please? I'm starving.'

'Don't spoil your tea,' she said.

'It won't,' I said, seizing a scone and buttering it lavishly. 'It's just to give me an appetite.'

'Ever such nice people they are,' chatted on my mother happily. 'Their name's Spencer. I invited Mrs Spencer round for a coffee earlier. Her husband's a policeman.'

I choked on my scone. Unlike some of the kids at school, I don't actively dislike the police, but one next door was, I felt, a bit much. I don't dislike elephants either but I wouldn't keep a herd in the back garden.

My mother noticed the choke but misinterpreted it.

'Don't gobble that scone, James,' she said. 'You'll get indigestion.'

Then she returned to the new neighbours' theme.

'A detective inspector he is,' she confided. 'That's quite high up.'

'A detective?' My interest quickened. Detectives were generally reckoned to be more glamorous than mere bobbies. In fact, though I'd recently gone off the idea, I had considered joining the CID myself when I grew up.

'And they've got a daughter,' continued my mother. 'Her name's Samantha. She's eleven. And she'll be going to your school. They've been down to see the head today. She's starting Monday.'

'Only eleven?' I said indistinctly, through a mouthful of scone. 'Just a bit of a kid then.'

'I said you'd take her to school on Monday morning,' said my mother blithely. 'Show her the ropes.'

I froze with the last mouthful of scone halfway to my mouth.

'You said what?'

'That you'd take her to school on Monday. Her mum was ever so pleased.'

'I'm taking no girl to school,' I said. 'I'd never hear the last of it.'

'Only the first morning, dear,' said my mother placidly. 'She'll be cycling there, same as you, so it won't hold you up.'

'I don't care,' I said. 'I'm not doing it.'

'I promised,' said my mother.

I knew at once I'd lost the battle. A promise, in our family, is sacred. If my mother had made a promise on my behalf, both my parents were going to combine to see that I upheld the family honour, as it were.

On Monday morning I was to be stuck with Samantha Spencer, whose father was a policeman. Fatso Austin and company were going to have a field day.

Gloomily I ate the last mouthful of scone.

When I met Polly on Saturday morning on my way

to the library, I broke the news of Samantha to him. He accepted it quite philosophically.

'It's only one morning, JB. And we can ditch her as soon as we get in the yard. You've only to take her as far as the school.'

I brightened.

'That's true,' I said. 'Once we're there we can ignore her. Perhaps no one will even notice.'

I didn't see anything of our new neighbours during Saturday, because, in the afternoon, my dad took Polly and me to the football match and, at night, I was glued to a really good film on telly. But, on Sunday morning, when I was kicking a football around in our back garden and trying to dribble it the way I'd seen the centre forward do the previous day, I heard, from next door's garden, this breathless laughter, interspersed with heavy thuds.

It sounded as if my imaginary herd of elephants had actually materialized.

I'm still not very tall, but I had found that, if I stood on tiptoe, I could just about see over the wall separating our garden from next door.

I stood on tiptoe.

They had a sort of padded mat thing spread out on the patio, and two figures, dressed in baggy white suits, were tossing each other all over it. The tiny figure with fair hair was obviously Samantha. The six-foot athletic-looking hunk, was, equally obviously, Detective Inspector Spencer. My final deduction, in my best Sherlock Holmes vein, was that he was teaching her judo.

Detectives must have some sort of sixth sense which warns them when they are being watched, because it was only about a minute later that the man paused, looked straight up at me and grinned.

'James Bond, I presume?'

'That's right,' I said. 'And you're Mr Spencer.'

'Correct. Allow me to introduce Samantha. It was so kind of you to offer to take her to school tomorrow.'

I opened my mouth to say I'd done no such thing. Then I shut it again. Mr Spencer's expression made it quite clear, to one of my intelligence, not only that he was aware that the offer hadn't come from me, but also that he was going to hold me to it.

So I just said: 'Hello, Samantha.' Awkwardly.

The girl gave a wide smile.

'Call me Sam. Everybody does.'

There seemed to be no quick answer to that, so I didn't attempt one.

'Do you know judo?' Mr Spencer asked.

'No,' I said. 'I wish I did.'

'Come over and join in the lesson,' he said.

'Daddy's a black belt,' added Samantha proudly.

I thought, fleetingly, that the evildoers in the neighbourhood might be in for a bit of a shock when they encountered Detective Inspector Spencer. I even wondered if he'd been specially drafted in to deal with Raffles.

'Well,' he said, 'are you coming?'

I hesitated no longer.

'Yeah!' I said. 'Ta.'

I scrambled ungracefully over the wall.

I should explain that our school, at the moment, is afflicted with two particularly nasty bullies. They're not, fortunately, in the same form as Polly and me. They're in the thickos' class actually, because they're what my dad calls 'all brawn and no brains', but they've got all the kids scared silly. To avoid being duffed up, kids hand over sweets, pocket money, and even prized possessions. I think the teachers know it goes on but can't prove it, because the two bullies have got us too terrified to split on them. Their names are Brian Mulvey (known as 'Big Brian') and Derek 'the Fist' Foster. And they make the Mafia look like it's wearing L-plates.

As I landed over the wall, I was thinking that a bit of judo was just what I needed to give these two beauties their comeuppance.

I was sent into the house, where Mrs Spencer provided me with one of those ill-fitting suits which seem obligatory for judo experts, then, when I emerged suitably clad, we plunged into the lesson right away. It was hard work, I can tell you. And also, I began to feel so *inadequate*. I mean, I'm not very big, but Samantha's head only reached my shoulder, and she was tossing me about all over that mat like a rag doll.

However, by the end of an hour's painful effort, I had learned how to fall properly and had practised one throw – which Mr Spencer said (disparagingly) might work if my opponent knew no judo at all.

Which Big Brian and 'the Fist' didn't!

I went in to lunch feeling as though I were well on the way to becoming a black belt myself.

After lunch I went round to Polly's place to try out his latest computer game. Honestly, his mum may be a fusspot, but, as I've mentioned, she spoils him dead rotten. His bedroom – which is quite large and more of a bedsit really – is so crammed with all his expensive gadgets, complete with software, that it

131

looks as if he might take off for Mars at any moment. His dad isn't a millionaire either. Just doting.

Anyway, when I told Polly I was learning judo ready to join the SAS when I grew up, he was quite impressed. And envious. He was pretty sure his mum wouldn't let him take the necessary risks involved in mastering this ancient art.

Next morning I found Samantha – and her bicycle – waiting outside our gate. She was wearing complete school uniform and a 'butter wouldn't melt' expression. The expression didn't deceive me for one moment. It may work against grown-ups, but it's absolutely useless when up against another habitual wearer.

'Right,' I said curtly. 'Come on.'

We set off.

On the way I proffered one piece of advice.

'I shouldn't let on about your dad being a policeman,' I told her.

'Why ever not?' asked Samantha.

After this rejection of my kindly meant counsel, we proceeded in silence.

Polly was just emerging from his front gate as we arrived. He greeted me, eyed Samantha warily and mounted his bike. As we were now meeting more traffic, we rode in single file, with me leading, Polly as the meat in the sandwich and Samantha bringing up the rear.

I began to feel like the leader of a baggage train crossing the Sahara.

Once through the school gates, I showed Samantha where to leave her bike and pointed out a group of girls who looked about the same age. Then Polly and I thankfully departed to rejoin the rest of our mob. I was grateful to observe that none of them seemed to have noticed our arrival with a small girl in tow.

I next saw Sam – as I must learn to call her – in the lunch hour. Not to speak to. She was on the other side of the yard. But I saw the dreaded Big Brian approaching her, with his sidekick in tow. Obviously he had noted a new little chicken ripe for the plucking.

I began to watch events with a certain hopeful interest.

Sam had just opened a box of chocolates and was offering them round to the other girls in the group. I saw Brian say something to her. I saw Sam shake her head. He stretched out a hand. She put the box behind her back. Brian made a grab for her. Sam suddenly made a quick movement – and Brian flew ungracefully over her left shoulder. He landed heavily and lay there, obviously wondering what had happened to him.

Like every other kid in the yard, Polly and I stood stock-still for a minute and then began to converge on the scene.

So did Mr Tilsley, a rather wet type of teacher, who was the poor sap on yard duty.

I heard him say: 'What's going on here?'

Sam pointed at Big Brian, who was now sitting up.

'I think he slipped,' she said.

Big Brian opened his mouth and then shut it again. I saw his difficulty. The terror of the school could hardly point to four feet six inches of schoolgirl and say, 'She threw me over her head.' His sidekick, too, appeared to have joined him in a vow of silence. They sloped off dismally. Sam beamed at Mr Tilsley and offered him a choc. He accepted it, smiling fatuously, and wandered on his aimless way. Sam was immediately surrounded by a cooing, admiring crowd of girls who began to behave as if she were their latest pop idol.

The bell went and we all drifted into school.

I didn't see Samantha for the rest of the afternoon. I had been afraid I'd find her waiting for Polly and me at four o'clock but she wasn't. I thought she'd probably been escorted home by her fan club.

After I'd left Polly, however, and was approaching our house, I saw her swinging on the Spencers' gate. As I dismounted from my bike she said:

'The other girls say you're quite a famous detective.'

I smirked modestly.

'Not exactly famous,' I said. 'Not yet.'

'They say you saved the PM from being assassinated.'

'True,' I said casually.

'And that you rescued a prince from being kidnapped.'

'That too,' I said.

'And knocked out a thug trying to steal a car.'

'I've done all those things,' I said.

'They say Polly Perkins is your second-in-command.'

'He is.'

'Well,' said Samantha, 'what I want to know is, can I be your third man?'

I gazed at her in open-mouthed horror. For a moment, unusually for me, words just wouldn't come.

'Well,' she said again, 'what about it?'

134

I recovered my powers of speech with a rush.

'No!' I said. 'No, you jolly well can't.'

'Why not?'

'Because you're a girl,' I said.

'What's that got to do with it?'

'Everything,' I said. 'We don't want women. They always mess things up.'

'I'd be jolly useful. I'd make a good hit man.'

'No,' I said.

'Is that final?'

'Absolutely,' I said, and waited for her to do the usual girlie thing of bursting into tears.

Sam didn't. She merely shrugged casually, climbed down from the gate and turned to go indoors, flinging one final remark over her shoulder as she went.

'You'll change your mind.'

Considerably shaken, I put my bike away and went indoors to tea.

After that, Samantha began to haunt Polly and me. I don't mean she tried to join in our games or anything. She was too subtle for that. But when we rode to school each morning, there she'd be, riding some way behind us. And, when we rode home at four o'clock, a quick glance round would reveal a determined, lonely little figure pedalling away further down the street. She never spoke or waved. She was just there. It was like being trailed by a singularly efficient bloodhound. Most unnerving we found it.

All of which didn't stop me going for my judo lesson the following Sunday. Sam and her father both greeted me most pleasantly, but, in the course of one bout, Samantha whispered:

'Changed your mind yet?'

'No,' I hissed.

She flung me casually to the floor and smiled down at me.

We woke the following morning to discover that our friendly neighbourhood Raffles had been busy once more. It was again reported on the eight o'clock news. This time his target really had been the Harringtons. Apparently he'd dismantled the burglar alarm, stolen some rather valuable pieces of porcelain, opened the safe and emptied it, and cut from its frame a picture said to be worth thousands. All without the sleeping family hearing a thing. It was most exciting.

As we rode to school Polly said:

'Heard about the burglary?'

'Yeah,' I said.

'You really ought to set out to trap him, JB. It's right up your street.'

'Not on your life,' I said. 'I've retired.'

Polly sighed.

'There's the tuck shop,' he said, changing the subject. 'Let's go in. I've run out of jelly babies.'

I should explain that this addiction to jelly babies is my friend's one vice.

Samantha followed us into the shop. She gave Polly's jelly babies a supercilious glance and purchased a bar of Toblerone. As we rode away, she was still on the trail.

We went into school.

After school that afternoon, as we entered the bike shed to collect our cycles, we saw Samantha pretending to adjust the chain on her bicycle. It was a ploy, of course. She was waiting to track us once again.

We ignored her and promptly broke a school rule by cycling straight across the yard and out through the gate. But it did us no good. A quick glance back as we reached the corner of the street showed the hound still on the scent.

'Can't we ditch her?' Polly asked desperately. 'She makes me nervous.'

It was at this moment I had the brilliant idea which I was to regret so bitterly later.

'Yeah,' I said. 'You know that empty house in Oak Street?'

Oak Street lay on our way home. It was a street of large, old-fashioned terraced houses, most of which looked as if they had seen better days. Many were now let off as flats, but, about the middle of the row, one had lain completely empty for months and was becoming increasingly tatty.

'Number thirteen,' said Polly. 'So what?'

'If we nip down the alley at the back of the houses,' I said, 'the back gate's off its hinges. I noticed when I was taking a short cut the other day. We could hide in the yard till she's gone.'

Polly hesitated.

'You know Mum doesn't like me going down back alleys. And it'll be dark soon.'

'We shan't be there long,' I said. 'Come on.'

I put on a bit of speed and shot off down the street. Polly, despite his doubts, followed. Samantha was temporarily out of sight round the corner. We turned into the alley, sped down it and went in through the gateway of number thirteen. Dismounting, we leaned our bikes against some dustbins in the yard and crouched behind the wall.

After a few minutes Polly said:

'D'you think she's gone now? Can we go home?'

I'd been looking at the house.

'Hang on a minute,' I said. 'Let's see if we can get inside.'

Empty houses have this sort of fascination for me. I always feel daring and adventurous exploring them – especially if they're old and a bit spooky.

This one looked all of that.

I guessed Polly was going to protest, so I didn't stop to listen. I just darted across to the back door of the house. I knew Polly would follow. He always does.

I tried the door. It swung silently open on remarkably well-oiled hinges, revealing a tiled passage behind.

'Come on,' I said.

We crept into the house and began to explore. The rooms were dirty and a bit cobwebby. I started to pretend I was a famous detective searching for a dead body.

Polly trailed unhappily behind me.

After a bit he said:

'Come on, JB. We've been all over. Sam must be home by now.'

I'd forgotten all about Samantha, but I was enjoying myself far too much to leave so tamely.

'We've not seen upstairs yet,' I said.

I began to climb the wide staircase. Polly uttered a sort of little moan, but followed obediently.

It was in the large back bedroom that we found the trunk. It stood in the middle of the floor, looking solid and uncompromising. Considering that, in my daydream, the detective had just discovered a headless corpse in a similar trunk, it gave me quite a start.

138

We stood and gazed at it in silence.

'It's the sort of thing that always has a body in it on telly,' Polly remarked.

Sometimes I think he goes in for mind-reading.

'We'd better look,' I said.

'Do we have to, JB?' Polly was on the way to the screaming hab-dabs again.

I was scared too, but in a way it was worse *not* knowing what was inside, if you see what I mean.

I stretched out a trembling hand and raised the lid just a little.

No headless corpse, anyway. But the trunk certainly wasn't empty.

I opened the lid more fully and investigated. Inside, there was a case like a rather large-sized document case, a rolled-up piece of canvas and some china ornaments.

Polly, peering agitatedly over my shoulder, let out a squeak.

'That's them!'

'What's what?' I said irritably.

'That ch-china.' Polly was beginning to stutter, so I knew he was excited. 'It l-looks like Mr Harrington's. I s-saw that p-piece when we were w-waiting in their hall after the b-bonfire.'

I looked more closely. Some of the ornaments did indeed look familiar.

'And,' said Polly, 'I bet that c-canvas is the stolen p-picture. It said on the news Raffles had c-cut it out of the frame.'

I unrolled the canvas.

It was a picture. A girl standing in a field of corn, it looked like.

'So I bet,' I said, 'that the money from the safe's in that case thing.'

I tried the metalled case. It was locked.

Polly, as usual, requested guidance.

'What shall we do, JB?'

Before I could answer I heard a sound from behind us and spun round. Two men stood in the doorway.

'What the hell are you kids doing here?' one of them asked.

Polly gave a little squeal of horror and clutched my arm. I didn't blame him. The two men in the doorway looked very ugly customers indeed.

The one who had spoken was a slim, dark bloke of medium height and he was sort of sinister-looking. Any TV producer would have cast him right away as the villain. The other thug was more like a gorilla than a man. He was huge – tall, and fat with it. His long arms hung down like a gorilla's and even his face bore out the likeness. In fact, he looked a natural to play the lead in any contemplated remake of 'King Kong'. I noticed, moreover, that both men looked annoyed and my heart began to thud unpleasantly.

'We're not doing anything,' I said, hoping he couldn't see my legs shaking. 'We're just going.'

I started to edge past, but Mr Sinister let out a snarl.

'You're going nowhere. Get them, Ben.'

King Kong made a grab. He got me in one large hand and Polly in the other and proceeded to shake us until our freckles rattled.

'Want me to croak 'em?' he asked.

Honestly, I thought people only said things like that on telly!

I prayed the answer would be a prompt, 'No.

140

Certainly not.' My heart sank when Mr Sinister said:

'Not here, you fool. We'll take them with us. Shove them against that wall.'

King Kong flung us at the far wall. We practically bounced off it.

'Take the trunk down to the van,' instructed Sinister. 'I'll keep an eye on them till you come back.'

'OK, boss.' King Kong shouldered the trunk and set off without apparent effort.

I transferred my gaze to Sinister. Polly was already looking at him like a rabbit mesmerized by a singularly vicious stoat. I saw why.

A gun had sprouted in Sinister's hand. It was pointed at us.

Really, I thought, this can't be happening. I must be having a nightmare.

Surreptitiously I pinched myself. It wasn't a nightmare. It was for real. I regretted my bright idea of the empty house. Even Samantha was better than this.

King Kong came back.

'I've loaded the trunk,' he said.

'Was anyone around?' asked Sinister.

'Not a soul. It's getting dark and beginning to rain.'

'Right,' said Sinister. 'Take these two kids down and shove 'em in the back with the stuff.'

'OK, boss.' King Kong grinned at us evilly, showing teeth that had lacked the attention of a dentist for a very long time. I suddenly remembered who he resembled – that 'Jaws' guy in some of the Bond films. I didn't have time to dwell on the likeness. He picked us both up – me under one vast arm and Polly under the other – and set off down the stairs.

I reflected bitterly that I'd not even had time to try out my one, painfully learned, judo throw. It would, in any case, have been like trying to throw the Empire State Building.

I began to kick his shins like mad but it had no apparent effect. Moreover, Sinister, following behind, hissed:

'Keep still, you stupid brat, or I'll bang you over the head.'

I saw he was still waving the gun about in an increasingly agitated fashion, so I desisted.

As we made our exit through the back door and across the filthy yard, I risked a quick glance up and down the alleyway.

No one in sight. Typical!

We were flung into the back of the van – a small, unmarked blue one, I noticed – and the doors were slammed, leaving us in complete darkness.

After a minute I heard the engine start up and felt the van begin to move.

'I've got a hole in the pocket of my anorak,' Polly said.

For a moment I thought the strain must have been too much for him and he'd gone bonkers.

'So what?' I said cautiously.

'Well, I've been pushing jelly babies out through it. They're all down the stairs in that rotten house. And I dropped some in the alley before that thug shoved us into the van. I thought it'd be like laying a trail if Sam came back to look for us. . . .'

His voice died away miserably. I forbore to tell him it was now pretty dark, that Sam would be safely at home wolfing her tea, and that any grown-up finding jelly babies in a back alley would simply think kids had been larking about.

But it did give me the germ of an idea. A faint, forlorn hope maybe, but it was better than sitting here worrying about what lay ahead.

As my eyes got used to the gloom, I noticed a hole in the near side of the van, down near the floor. Only a very small hole it was, but big enough for what I had in mind.

'Have you got any left?' I said.

'Any what?'

'Jelly babies, you moron.'

'Oh yes, lots. I think the man gave me overweight,' said Polly seriously.

His mind tends to fish up irrelevant details at unsuitable moments.

'I've got my diary in my pocket,' I said. 'I'll tear out some pages and print SOS on each. Then you wrap one round each jelly baby and keep shoving them out of the van through that hole.'

'Brill!' said Polly fervently. 'I knew you'd think of something, JB.'

I grunted. Personally, I thought we were backing a loser. But we had to do something.

It's harder than you think to print SOS with a biro on a small piece of paper in a dark and joggling van, but I kept on struggling. Polly, meanwhile, kept shoving the parcelled babies through the hole. It seemed to go on a very long time – and the van was still travelling.

It was travelling quite quickly too, I thought. We couldn't still be in the town, moving at this speed and never stopping for traffic lights or anything. Not that that brilliant deduction was likely to do us any good.

At last Polly said: 'I've run out of jelly babies.'

'That's it then,' I said gloomily.

'Couldn't we just throw the pieces of paper out?'

'They'd blow away,' I said. 'No good as a trail.'

'JB,' said Polly anxiously, 'are they really going to kill us?'

'I don't know,' I said.

'On telly,' said Polly bitterly, 'we'd be rescued any time now.'

Without warning, the van suddenly lurched across the road, flinging us into a tangled heap on the floor. There was a sound like a tyre bursting or something, and a lot of shouting. The van skidded to a halt. There were a couple more bangs. Then a voice yelled:

'Are you kids all right in there?'

I removed Polly's foot from my mouth and shouted:

'Yeah. We're OK.'

'Jolly good,' said the voice reassuringly. 'Hang on. We'll have you out of there in a brace of shakes.'

The sounds of what appeared to be a pitched battle going on outside were replaced by something battering on the doors of the van. They burst open. Torches were shone on to us, almost blinding us. Behind the torches we saw uniformed figures.

Police! In that moment I knew what exiles mean when they say they're glad to see a British bobby.

'Are you hurt?' asked a voice from outside.

'Not a bit,' I said, trying to sound calm and casual, and failing very badly.

Willing hands helped us out of the van. I looked round. Three police cars. *Loads* of police. And, oh joy, Mr Sinister and King Kong, in handcuffs, being thrust (ungently) into two separate cars.

144

Another car screeched to a halt by us. Out of it climbed Detective Inspector Spencer, followed by another fattish guy, also in plain clothes – Detective Sergeant Mills, no less. Sharon's dad.

'James,' said Detective Inspector Spencer, 'are you both OK?'

'Fine,' I said. 'Did you find the trail we'd laid for you?'

He looked puzzled.

'What trail?'

'Jelly babies,' said Polly.

He looked even more puzzled – as well he might. I explained. His face cleared.

'Sorry, no,' he said. 'Though, of course,' he added hastily, 'it was pretty quick-witted of you to think of it. You certainly kept your cool.'

'How did you find us then?' I asked curiously.

'Oh, that was Samantha. She'd followed you. I gather it was some sort of game you were all playing, wasn't it?'

'No,' said Polly.

I kicked him. Surreptitiously, of course.

'That's right,' I said.

'Well, after you'd hidden in the empty house, she hung about outside for a bit, waiting for you to emerge. Then she saw the van back into the alleyway and two men get out and go into the house. She thought you might be in danger, so she hid behind a dustbin and watched. When she saw the man carry you out and bundle you into the van, she knew you'd got trouble. So she noted the number of the van, and, as soon as it had driven off, she grabbed her bike, got to the nearest phone box and rang me. We put out a general alert for the van. The rest you know.'

'So it was Sam, not our trail, that led you to us,' Polly said in a deflated sort of way.

'You did very well anyway.' Detective Inspector Spencer was trying to be kind, which was annoying. But I still had an ace to play.

'By the way,' I said casually, 'all the stuff stolen from the Harringtons last night is in a trunk in the van.'

'What?' He sounded suitably startled. 'Just have a dekko, Constable, will you?'

A uniformed figure leapt for the van. A minute later he reappeared looking excited.

'He's right, sir. It's all here.'

'Well, well, well!' Detective Inspector Spencer gazed down at me. I gazed back triumphantly. Let Samantha beat that.

'Well done, lads,' he said. Appreciative murmurs came from all round us. I began to feel better.

'I'd better get you two home.' He turned to Sharon's dad. 'Carry on here, Sergeant, will you?'

'Right, sir.' Detective Sergeant Mills, obviously drunk with a sense of divine power, began giving orders left, right and centre.

We were bundled into Detective Inspector Spencer's car and driven away.

Polly's mum was having hysterics in our lounge when we arrived. My own mother and a young policewoman were trying to calm her. Both dads stood helplessly by.

As we entered, Polly's mum sort of rushed at him with arms outstretched, but he sidestepped behind Detective Inspector Spencer, who almost suffered the full force of the embrace. Then, of course, there were explanations and recriminations and congratu-

146

lations, and eventually Polly and his clucking parents departed.

Detective Inspector Spencer stayed only long enough to assure my parents that my help had been invaluable in recovering the stolen property, then he too got up to leave.

'Was one of those two men Raffles?' I asked.

'I don't think so,' he said. 'Their job was simply to collect the loot.'

'Then you still haven't caught Raffles?'

'We shall,' he said. 'They'll tell us all about him.'

'Sing like canaries,' I said, just to show him I'd taken the trouble to learn the lingo.

Later that evening, I was finishing my belated tea when the phone rang. My mother went to answer it. A minute or so later she came back.

'James,' she said, 'it's Samantha Spencer for you. I think she wants to say she's glad you're safe.'

I didn't think that was at all what Samantha wanted to say, and I was right.

'Good job I noted the number of that van, wasn't it?'

'Yeah,' I said.

'I reckon I saved your life.'

'Yeah. Thanks,' I said.

'So now can I be your third man?'

What could I do? Trapped in a catch-22 situation. There was a pause.

'OK,' I said at last. 'You're in. But you obey orders, see?'

'Of course, James.' Sam was almost purring. 'So long – Chief. See you tomorrow.'

'See you,' I said.

I put the phone down and returned to my meal.

After all, Sam wasn't bad, I thought. And, after her summary treatment of Big Brian and 'the Fist', her own score at school was pretty high.

As a threesome we'd be invincible.

Moreover, there was another possible advantage.

I was wondering whether her dad would put in a good word for me with the police hierarchy when I left school. I had again determined that my future career lay at Scotland Yard.

9

The Adventure of the Sinful Santa

The last week of the Christmas term proved to be the usual hectic rush, with the teachers all getting snappier and snappier as the season of goodwill approached. For two nights in the week the Drama Club were doing a sort of rock musical version of *A Christmas Carol*, written by a couple of the teachers. I had hoped to be cast as Scrooge or Bob Cratchit, but, as one of the smallest boys in the group, I was inevitably stuck with Tiny Tim, an incrediby soppy type of child, in my opinion. It was a rotten part and I hated it because it did nothing for my image, but I lacked the guts to stand there and tell Mrs Wallis, 'the Walrus', who was producing the thing, that I didn't want to be in it. So I suffered it, and told everyone that I was only doing it to show what a versatile actor I was, as they would see me in quite a different role on telly on Boxing Day.

This, of course, was my Sark adventure, which was to be screened at last. I was really looking forward to the furore that would cause – both at school and with my still disbelieving parents.

However, a whole lot was to happen before Boxing Day, as you will see.

The last few days of school were chaotic and they really flew. The musical was a great success. Even my parents enjoyed it, and they're not rock addicts by any stretch of the imagination. Then, the next night, came the Christmas party, which was a bit of a dead bore really, but the nosh was super – sausage rolls and hamburgers and meat pies and hot dogs and crisps and pop. The lot. I felt sick all night but it was worth it.

Finally came the best moment of all – four o'clock Friday. We all whooped our way out of the school gates to two and a half weeks of glorious freedom. With, of course, the excitements of Christmas (and my TV appearance) thrown in.

My parents had originally promised to take me to London the following day – Saturday – so that we could do our Christmas shopping in Oxford Street and see the lights and the tree and everything. However, this trip was now off. There'd been a number of bomb scares from various terrorist groups over the past ten days or so. Not just scares either. Two bombs had actually gone off. One in Harrods (of course) and the other in Marks and Spencer in Oxford Street. No one had been killed or even seriously hurt, but there had been threats that the campaign would be stepped up in the final days before Christmas.

My mother, who had been becoming edgier ever since the news of the first explosion, finally did a Mrs Perkins on us and announced that our trip was too dangerous and must be cancelled forthwith. To counteract my disappointment, my parents then told me that, to make up, they'd buy me the new BMX bike I'd been hankering after, as a Christmas present. This meant more to me than any trip to London and I was over the moon about it. My father was pleased too. He hates London. And my mother was delighted at having saved her family from death at the hands of bomb-crazed terrorists.

So we were all happy, except that I still had to find presents for Mum and Dad. To say nothing of our Susan, Auntie May, Polly, and now Samantha. I'd been saving up for weeks and had hoped to get the lot in one fell swoop in London. Now it looked as if I'd have to search around locally.

About eight o'clock on Friday evening, however, Sam came round to say her dad was taking her to Camcaster the following morning and would we like a lift in. We could separate for the morning, she said, to do our shopping, then all meet up for lunch, and later her dad would bring us home.

This sounded a good idea. My parents approved and even Polly's mum couldn't see any dangers, as her son would be with a representative of the forces of law and order for most of the day.

So it was arranged that Polly should be at our house the following morning for a nine o'clock start.

I broke open my money box and found that, though I wasn't yet in the millionaire bracket, I did have enough money not only to keep the wolf from the door, but to offer him a few sips of champagne if he arrived. If I was careful over my gift-buying, I thought, I might even have a little something left over for myself.

The next morning was cold and frosty, but skies were clear and there was the promise of a bright, sunny day. By ten minutes to nine, I was outside our gate, looking anxiously up the road for Polly. He came puffing up ten minutes later, dressed as if he were accompanying Scott to the South Pole. He was

151

even wearing a little knitted cap, which he thrust hastily into his pocket as soon as he saw me.

I didn't comment. I know he has to do these things to keep his mum happy.

Inspector Spencer's a pretty good driver – better than my dad really. Being a policeman, he does have to take more notice of speed limits, to avoid letting the side down. He's good company, too, for an oldie, and during the journey we learned quite a bit about some of his more successful cases.

I mentioned that I thought of becoming Assistant Commissioner at Scotland Yard when I grew up, and he was very interested and gave me all sorts of helpful tips. As we neared Camcaster, he said:

'Where are you two making for?'

'Creasey's,' I said. 'We can do all our shopping there and get it out of the way, then p'raps go in the park.'

'Right,' he said. 'In that case, we'll lunch in Creasey's restaurant. Meet you there at quarter to one.'

'OK,' I said. 'Super.'

He dropped us off near the store and we stood waving goodbye to Sam until the car turned the corner, then we rushed off and tried to surprise the glass door of the shop by diving at it suddenly, but, as always, it was ready for us.

If you think that sounds funny, perhaps I should explain that Creasey's has one of those automatic doors which opens as you approach it. It doesn't matter how you vary your speed or anything, that door can out-think you. It's a pretty good store really, with four floors and a basement – which houses a restaurant – and is what my mum calls a 'classy shop'. There are other big stores in Camcaster, like Asda and Marks and Spencer and so on, but we both knew our mums would appreciate a present gift-wrapped by Creasey's. It would sort of show we cared. It would also save our messing about with Sellotape and fancy paper later.

'My mum wants perfume, I know,' Polly said, 'but I can't remember what sort she likes.'

'Perhaps you'll know it when you see it,' I said.

'I'll know it when I *smell* it. I'll just have to try them all till I find it. Can I try them on you, JB?'

'No,' I said. Firmly.

So we wandered round the perfume counter, with Polly spraying himself with various scents, until a shop assistant came up and said rudely:

'You two kids stop messing about and get out.'

I looked at her coldly.

'We are trying,' I said, 'to make a purchase. It's a present for a lady.'

She looked a bit doubtful at that, but fortunately, at that moment, Polly waved a bottle in the air and shouted:

'Got it!'

The assistant at once became more helpful.

'Is that the one you want?'

'Sure is,' said Polly, fishing in his anorak pocket for his wallet.

'What size of bottle?'

'About a pint, I suppose,' said Polly vaguely.

The assistant looked a bit bewildered, but eventually we got that one sorted out and Polly left triumphantly with a beautifully gift-wrapped parcel.

As I knew my mum wanted a silk scarf and as everyone else was going to get either soap or hankies whether they wanted them or not, we managed the rest of our shopping with comparative ease. We'd finished the lot just after half-eleven, which left us over an hour to fill in before lunch.

We shot down to the basement on the escalator, so that we could drool over the menu on the restaurant door and decide what we were going to eat later. After a bit, however, a uniformed commissionaire appeared and snapped:

'What are you two up to?'

I gave him my withering glare. He remained unwithered.

'We're lunching here with friends later,' I said loftily.

'Then get off out of it till later,' advised the commissionaire.

He looked a bit big, and nasty with it, so we went.

'Let's go up to the top floor,' suggested Polly. 'There'll be lots to look at up there.'

Every Christmas the top floor at Creasey's becomes the toy floor. It's where Father Christmas lives in his grotto, dispensing toys to squalling tinies who never seem to get the present they want. There's always a big Christmas tree too, and people put parcels of discarded toys underneath it to be collected on Christmas Eve for the local children's home. It's always dead good, that toy floor, and, while Polly and I are now too grown-up to fancy rocking horses and toy cars and the like, it certainly still holds some fascination for us.

'Brill idea!' I said. 'Let's go up in the express lift.'

This was fun too, because the lift was one you worked yourself. So we got in and I became Captain Kirk and Polly was Spock, and we shot up and down a few times without letting the doors open for anyone else to get in. Then, on our third journey to the basement, we saw the big commissionaire glowering in through the glass at us, so we shot off again to the top floor and alighted.

Never push your luck, has always been my motto.

The display was as good as ever and we had a super time wandering around. First, we leered in through the door of the grotto, where a flustered Santa was trying to placate a tiny who'd asked for a tricycle and been given a rubber duck. Then Polly tried his hand at rodeo riding on a rocking horse. But we saw a floorwalker bearing down on us and looking grim, so Polly climbed down and we smarmed the assistant up by saying that our parents were considering buying the thing for Polly's kid sister. The bloke grew quite matey after that, and insisted on pressing various brochures about the joys of rocking horses into our unwilling hands. Finally we escaped and began to make our way across to the tree, which stood, in all its glory, at one end of the store.

Suddenly Polly said: 'That's funny!'

'What is?' I asked.

'I never knew Creasey's had *two* Santas.'

'They haven't.'

'They must have. Look!'

I looked. Father Christmas, in his full-dress uniform, was just crossing the floor towards the tree. He wasn't, I noticed, lumbered with the usual sack. He had just one package, gift-wrapped, which he carried carefully in both hands and laid at the foot of the tree as if it were a sacrificial offering. Then he turned and moved across to the down escalator. As he did so, he passed quite close to us. He gave us a smile, said 'Merry Christmas' and moved on.

'Funny!' said Polly again.

'Perhaps he's come out of the grotto,' I suggested, 'just to put that gift there for the kids' home.'

'No. It's not the same man. The Santa in the grotto was fatter. Besides, this one was wearing a big ring on his right hand. Like a heavy sort of signet thing. The Santa in the grotto had no rings. I noticed when he was struggling with that yelling kid.'

Polly does notice things like that. It probably comes of being a trained Cub Scout when he was young.

'Let's go and see what he's put under the tree, then,' I said.

We strolled over.

The present lay invitingly where Santa had placed it; an oblong package, about the size of a shoe box, wrapped in colourful paper patterned all over with holly and fat robins and with a red bow on top. There was no card attached that I could see.

'Fancy some moron giving those kids in the home an alarm clock,' Polly said. 'That's no sort of present.'

I frowned at him.

'How d'you know someone's given them an alarm clock? You got X-ray eyes or something?'

'No,' said Polly simply. 'I can hear it ticking.'

'Ticking?'

'Yes. In one of those parcels.'

I listened. The lad was right. From the pile of parcels under the tree, there came a gentle, regular tick.

I bent down to try and isolate it. I succeeded. The

ticking came from Santa's box. I stood up again rather hastily, thoughts of our cancelled London visit racing round my agile mind.

'It's a bomb,' I said. 'Santa's planted a time bomb.'

'A bomb?' Polly's voice rose to a falsetto squeak. 'Are you sure, JB?'

'I'm sure,' I said.

I wasn't, actually. It seemed so far-fetched. I mean – in dozy old Camcaster! It couldn't be! But suppose it was?

Polly's next question was inevitable.

'What shall we do, JB?'

'We'd better tell someone,' I said. 'Sharpish.'

'Is it going to go off right away?'

I glared at him.

'How do I know, you clot? Look, there's an assistant over there. Come on.'

A middle-aged woman who looked like a bad imitation of Molly Sugden in 'Are You Being Served?' was moving in our direction. We trotted over to her.

'Excuse me,' I said.

She took about as much notice of me as if I'd been a dead duck. Her gaze was fixed beyond us on a couple with two small children, who had paused by the rocking horse in an interested sort of way.

'Excuse me,' I repeated.

'Later,' she hissed. Then she turned the full force of her synthetic smile on the prospective buyers.

'If that thing could go off any minute, why don't we tell someone outside?' Polly said plaintively.

He had a point.

I will say this for Polly, you know. He may not be

157

one of the world's greatest brains, but he has a terrifically well-developed sense of self-preservation.

'Good thinking,' I said. 'Let's go down to the car park and see if Detective Inspector Spencer's here yet.'

We galloped off in the direction of the down escalator. Somehow I didn't feel like hanging about waiting for the lift to come up.

We ran all the way down the escalator. It was moving, of course, but somehow it seemed slower than usual.

Once on the ground floor, I said: 'Back door. It leads straight on to the car park.'

The back door was a revolving one. In our state of mind, we didn't even whirl round several times as we usually did. We just wanted out.

Our luck was in. At the far side of the car park, Detective Inspector Spencer and Samantha had just alighted from their car.

'There he is!' I said.

'And there's Santa,' said Polly.

I looked round. No Santa was visible.

'Are you seeing things?' I said.

'No. That man who came out after us, carrying a suitcase. He's not dressed like Santa now, but he's wearing the same ring. Look! There he goes.'

I followed the direcon of Polly's pointing finger.

A stockily built, grey-haired man, with a pale, spotty face, was just crossing the car park. He was moving quite swiftly and seemed to be heading for the far end, where the Spencers' car was parked.

'Are you going to let him get away, JB?' Polly sounded disappointed.

Suddenly a bright idea struck me. It wasn't very original, actually. I'd seen it used in a thriller on TV

158

the previous evening. In the film it had worked well.

I raised my right arm and pointed dramatically at the ex-Santa.

'Stop, thief!' I shrieked.

I may say, at this point, that either the great British public don't watch enough telly or they're just naturally slow on the uptake. In the film, a general chase had followed that simple remark. In real life things were quite different. A few people looked round, one or two laughed, one elderly man remarked, 'Stupid brats', and a yobbo type on the sidelines cheered ironically. No one made any move to help.

'Stop, thief!' I shouted again.

I was beginning to feel a bit silly. Suppose Polly had been wrong and the poor bloke wasn't the fake Santa Claus at all, but just some law-abiding citizen going about his daily pursuits?

James Bond – prime wally again. Back, down the longest snake on the board, to square one.

It was then that our quarry made his first mistake. He began to run. And it was also then that Sam proved her worth as third man. As Santa rushed past her, she stuck out a small foot. . . .

Santa went flying. He dropped his suitcase, which was neatly fielded by Samantha. A firm hand helped him to his feet. I was pleased to notice that the hand, which belonged to Detective Inspector Spencer, retained its grip even when the man was upright.

'Come on,' I said to Polly. 'Let's explain.'

We galloped over to Sam, her father and the captive Santa, round whom a small group was beginning to form. I saw a uniformed policeman

159

approaching somewhat ponderously across the car park to join in the fun.

We got there first.

'I assure you that the child is mistaken,' 'Santa' was saying. 'Please let me go, Mr – er –'

'Detective Inspector Spencer,' said Sam's dad gently. 'And I must insist, sir, that you remain till this is sorted out.' He looked at me. 'Has he robbed you, James?'

'No,' I said. 'But he's put a bomb under the Christmas tree in Creasey's.'

My voice has always carried well. I heard a gasp and a rustle from the crowd, and several of our audience melted away in double-quick time.

Detective Inspector Spencer looked at me.

'Is this your stupid idea of a joke, James?'

'No,' I said. 'He was dressed as Santa, but there was already one in Creasey's and they'd never have two and he put a parcel which ticked under the tree. It's still there.'

The man gave a forced laugh.

'The child is out of his mind, Inspector. Probably he has been glue-sniffing. I am, in fact, a sales rep. Which is why I have just been visiting Creasey's.'

Detective Inspector Spencer hesitated. I could see the doubts beginning to crowd in. I felt desperate.

Polly, his stammer well in evidence, spoke out.

'If you're a s-sales rep why is there a S-santa costume in your s-suitcase?'

'Open the case, sir,' said Detective Inspector Spencer politely. 'We'll soon sort this out.'

There was a long pause. The police constable, who had now arrived, cleared his throat in a portentous fashion. Otherwise, the silence was absolute.

Reluctantly the man produced a key from his trouser pocket. Even more reluctantly he unlocked the suitcase.

Another pause.

'Open it, please, sir.' Detective Inspector Spencer's politeness never wavered.

The man flung back the lid. Large black boots were revealed, together with a white beard, lying on top of a scarlet, fur-trimmed tunic.

The ex-Santa gave a desperate wriggle to escape. With anyone else he might have managed it. Of course, the poor sap didn't know he was in the hands of a judo expert. In a moment he stood helpless, with one arm twisted up behind his back in what appeared to be an extremely uncomfortable position.

Detective Inspector Spencer looked at me.

'Sure about the bomb, James?'

'Yes,' I said.

Polly nodded vigorously and made his affirmative noise.

Sam's dad became all official. He waved his ID card at the constable and instructed him to get on to the station pronto on his walkie-talkie and report a suspect bomb in Creasey's. He finished by snapping the words: 'Jump to it, man,' in a sergeant-major type of voice which had the constable attempting to move faster than the speed of sound.

After this, things began to happen very quickly indeed.

Police cars, with sirens blaring, started to appear all over the car park. Uniformed police rushed into the shop. Loudspeakers advised people to leave the store as quickly as possible but without panic. Police escorted customers out. We were moved from the car

161

park into a side street. The area was cordoned off. A depressed and swearing ex-Santa was driven off in a police car. It was just all go and very exciting.

Except that I was getting more and more worried, because, of course, I wasn't at all sure it was a bomb. I mean, Camcaster isn't London by any manner of means. A right couple of idiots Polly and I were going to look if some moron had put an alarm clock in one of those parcels. I remembered the awful fiasco of the unmasking of Evelyn Smythe. I remembered my daring rescue of a non-kidnap victim. I remembered the murder-that-never-was. And I began to feel sick. I knew Polly was worried too because he'd gone all fidgety and he kept looking at me in a depressed sort of way, like a spaniel wondering whether it's brought Master the right slippers.

Tense minutes ticked by.

At last a grim-faced policeman, wearing a rather superior sort of uniform well decorated with gold braid and things, came towards us. He gave Detective Inspector Spencer a brief and meaningful nod.

Well, of course I guessed what that meant. I dug Polly in the ribs to make sure he'd got the message. But he'd lost his sad spaniel look, so I knew that he had.

Then the army arrived.

Now I was sure there really was a bomb, I began to find the whole thing fascinating. We all craned our necks to see what was going on and I was a bit disappointed we couldn't get any closer – though glad too in a way, naturally. Anyway, we hung around, expecting a bang, or flames, or both, any minute. Nothing happened, however, and after a time the soldiers – bomb-disposal experts, I suppose

– came out again. Then the police told us that the bomb had been safely defused but we couldn't go back in the store as they were going over the whole building with sniffer dogs in case our bomb hadn't been the only one.

The superior-type policeman came over to us again.

'Well done, Spencer,' he said. 'You averted what could have been a very nasty incident. What gave you the tip-off?'

'Nothing to do with me, sir,' said Sam's father. 'These two boys spotted the man planting the bomb and managed to trap him.'

Superior Type looked down at us.

'Congratulations, boys,' he said. 'What made you so sure it was a bomb?'

'It was ticking,' I said. 'And then it was funny, you see. Two Santas in one store.'

'You did a great job,' he said. 'We could do with more people like you. Are you going to join the Force when you grow up?'

'I sure am,' I said. 'I aim to be Assistant Commissioner at Scotland Yard.'

Superior Type and Sam's dad both laughed – but nicely, you know. Then Superior Type said:

'In that case, perhaps you'd like me to arrange for the two of you to have a guided tour of police headquarters in Camcaster during your Christmas holidays?'

'Rather!' I said. 'That would be fab.'

'Brill!' echoed Polly.

'Are you hoping to join the police too, Paul?' asked Sam's dad.

'In a way,' said Polly seriously. 'I want to be a pathologist.'

163

'Jolly good,' said Superior Type. 'We'll arrange that visit then. I'll just note down your names and addresses.'

'His name's James Bond, believe it or not,' said Detective Inspector Spencer, gesturing towards me.

This announcement caused the usual disbelieving chortles, but I've schooled myself now to remain deadpan throughout.

After that we were interviewed by the press and photographed by a TV team who had arrived out of nowhere, and eventually we got a belated lunch – not at Creasey's though, as it was still cordoned off. Then Sam's dad took us home.

On the way Sam said: 'Told you I'd be a useful third man. You'd never have caught Santa without me, you know.'

'Suppose not,' I said.

'And I let you take all the credit, didn't I?'

'Well, I found the bomb,' I said.

'I was the one who heard it ticking and spotted Santa's ring,' said Polly plaintively.

'All right. All right,' I said irritably. 'We're a good team, I'm not denying that. But I'm number one man.'

'Of course,' said Polly loyally. 'No one can hold a candle to you, JB. You're just brill, mate.'

'Tell me one thing though,' I said. 'How did you know Santa had his costume in that suitcase?'

'I didn't,' said Polly. 'It just seemed likely so I risked it.'

'You're coming on,' I said. 'That was pretty good.'

'Gosh! Thanks, JB!' said Polly fervently.

Samantha merely gave her pitying, Mona Lisa smile.

When I got home Mum said: 'Had a good day, dear?'

'Rather,' I said. 'I trapped a terrorist planting a bomb in Creasey's.'

My father looked up from his paper.

'James, you're romancing again,' he said warningly.

'I'm not,' I said. 'It was Santa Claus, see? Only there were two of him. One had this bomb. And he put it under the tree. And then –'

'Don't be silly, dear,' said my mother placidly. 'Go and wash your hands before tea.'

I sighed wearily but I didn't argue.

After all, I reasoned, I just had to make sure the whole family watched the six o'clock news on telly, when my bomb adventure was bound to be reported. Then, when they started exclaiming, 'Oh, look! That's our James,' I could just shrug and be all casual and dismissive about the whole affair. I didn't expect them to apologize, of course. Just grovel.

Looking back, I thought I'd interviewed pretty well: intelligent and caring with it. I wondered if my spots would show up much on our colour telly. Maybe they'd just look like freckles. I could hardly wait for six o'clock.

In fact, these Christmas holidays promised to be really fantastic from start to finish: two TV appearances and a guided tour of police headquarters as a real VIP and, to crown it all, a BMX bike.

James Bond, I thought, you've made it to the top. Here's to more crime-busting!

Other great reads from **Red Fox**

Further Red Fox titles that you might enjoy reading are listed on the following pages. They are available in bookshops or they can be ordered directly from us.

If you would like to order books, please send this form and the money due to:

ARROW BOOKS, BOOKSERVICE BY POST, PO BOX 29, DOUGLAS, ISLE OF MAN, BRITISH ISLES. Please enclose a cheque or postal order made out to Arrow Books Ltd for the amount due, plus 22p per book for postage and packing, both for orders within the UK and for overseas orders.

NAME _____

ADDRESS _____

_____

Please print clearly.

Whilst every effort is made to keep prices low, it is sometimes necessary to increase cover prices at short notice. If you are ordering books by post, to save delay it is advisable to phone to confirm the correct price. The number to ring is THE SALES DEPARTMENT 071 (if outside London) 973 9700.

Other great reads from **Red Fox**

Adventure Stories from Enid Blyton

THE ADVENTUROUS FOUR

A trip in a Scottish fishing boat turns into the adventure of a lifetime for Mary and Jill, their brother Tom and their friend Andy, when they are wrecked off a deserted island and stumble across an amazing secret. A thrilling adventure for readers from eight to twelve.

ISBN 0 09 9477009 £2.50

THE ADVENTUROUS FOUR AGAIN

'I don't expect we'll have any adventures *this* time,' says Tom, as he and sisters Mary and Jill arrive for another holiday. But Tom couldn't be more mistaken, for when the children sail along the coast to explore the Cliff of Birds with Andy the fisher boy, they discover much more than they bargained for . . .

ISBN 0 09 9477106 £2.50

COME TO THE CIRCUS

When Fenella's Aunt Jane decides to get married and live in Canada, Fenella is rather upset. And when she finds out that she is to be packed off to live with her aunt and uncle at Mr Crack's circus, she is horrified. How will she ever feel at home there when she is so scared of animals?

ISBN 0 09 937590 7 £1.75

Other great reads from **Red Fox**

**Discover the exciting and hilarious books of
Hazel Townson!**

THE MOVING STATUE

One windy day in the middle of his paper round, Jason Riddle
is blown against the town's war memorial statue.

But the statue moves its foot! Can this be true?

ISBN 0 09 973370 6   £1.99

ONE GREEN BOTTLE

Tim Evans has invented a fantasic new board game called
REDUNDO. But after he leaves it at his local toy shop it
disappears! Could Mr Snyder, the wily toy shop owner have
stolen the game to develop it for himself? Tim and his friend
Doggo decide to take drastic action and with the help of a
mysterious green bottle, plan a Reign of Terror.

ISBN 0 09 956810 1   £1.50

THE SPECKLED PANIC

When Kip buys Venger's Speckled Truthpaste instead of
toothpaste, funny things start happening. But they get out of
control when the headmaster eats some by mistake. What terrible
truths will he tell the parents on speech day?

ISBN 0 09 935490 X   £1.75

THE CHOKING PERIL

In this sequel to *The Speckled Panic*, Herbie, Kip and Arthur
Venger the inventor attempt to reform Grumpton's litterbugs.

ISBN 0 09 950530 4   £1.25

Other great reads from Red Fox

Discover the great animal stories of Colin Dann

JUST NUFFIN

The Summer holidays loomed ahead with nothing to look forward to except one dreary week in a caravan with only Mum and Dad for company. Roger was sure he'd be bored.

But then Dad finds Nuffin: an abandoned puppy who's more a bundle of skin and bones than a dog. Roger's holiday is transformed and he and Nuffin are inseparable. But Dad is adamant that Nuffin must find a new home. Is there *any* way Roger can persuade him to change his mind?

ISBN 0 09 966900 5   £1.99

KING OF THE VAGABONDS

'You're very young,' Sammy's mother said, 'so heed my advice. Don't go into Quartermile Field.'

His mother and sister are happily domesticated but Sammy, the tabby cat, feels different. They are content with their lot, never wondering what lies beyond their immediate surroundings. But Sammy is burningly curious and his life seems full of mysteries. Who is his father? Where has he gone? And what is the mystery of Quartermile Field?

ISBN 0 09 957190 0   £2.50